Belle's

ISBN: 978-1-932926-12-5

Artemesia Publishing, LLC
9 Mockingbird Hill Rd
Tijeras, New Mexico 87059
info@artemesiapublishing.com
www.apbooks.net

Attention humane societies, animal shelters and pet rescue clubs: Save 40% off the retail price of this book and use it for fund-raisers, premiums or gifts to your members. Please contact the publisher for details.

Attention school counselors, teachers, home schoolers and parents: Download a FREE copy of the Belle's Trial Activity Book from our website. This useful tool is ideal for small group counseling and classroom guidance activities. In addition, the learning activities provide wonderful opportunities for families to work together on a joint project that promotes stronger family ties and benefits the community.
http://www.apbooks.net

Library of Congress Cataloging-in-Publication Data
Gotsch, Connie, 1948-
Belle's trial / by Connie Gotsch ; illustrated by John Cogan.
p. cm.
Summary: Belle the dog's misbehavior while Darcy is at school has become a problem, but agility training, while challenging for both of them, helps teach Belle self-discipline and Darcy the importance of second chances.
ISBN 978-1-932926-12-5
[1. Dogs--Training--Fiction. 2. Pets--Fiction. 3. Human-animal relationships--Fiction. 4. Interpersonal relations--Fiction.] I. Cogan, John, 1953- ill. II. Title.
PZ7.G69376Bem 2010
[Fic]--dc22
2010035227

First Printing

Belle's Trial

By

Connie Gotsch

Illustrated By

John Cogan

Kinkajou Press
Albuquerque, New Mexico
www.apbooks.net

Awards and Praise for Belle's Star

First Place 2010 Juvenile Fiction National Federation of Press Women Communication Contest

First Place 2010 New Mexico Press Womens Communication Contest

2009 & 2010 New Mexico Book Award Finalist (Juvenile Book grade school to junior high)

Winner Silver Recipient: 2010 Mom's Choice Award® for Juvenile Level 2 Books (Ages 9 to 12)

"I highly recommend this book for all children who love animals and especially for children who have suffered abuse, bullying or other difficult situations in their homes and who need to learn to trust." ~ Nancy Marano, editor, PETroglyphs (www.petroglyphsnm.org)

Acknowledgments

Thanks to Uma Krishnaswami whose guidance made Belle's Trial possibly, the San Juan Writer's Group who critiqued it as it developed, the San Juan County 4-H Pooch Patrol for answering questions about dog agility and above all, thanks to Kiri, the inspiration for Belle.

To the memory of Gwen Spencer who started the whole process.

Table of Contents

Chapter 1

The Great Escape

The screech made me jump so high that all four feet left the ground. Flying out of my jaws, the ball I'd just caught smacked the wall of the human den.

"Belle, be careful." Buster barked. "That thing just missed the window."

A second and third wail drowned his warning. Diving into the bushes I stuck my head into a hole in the ground.

He slithered after me. "Those are police sirens. You know they won't hurt you. Holy dog biscuits."

"They're hurting my ears," I growled, burrowing deeper. "They make me wonder what bad human's out there doing something to poor dogs like us."

"You know most people aren't bad," Buster reasoned.

The wails moved down the street, fading as they went. My ears began to feel better. I lifted my head and shook dirt off my face.

"Sirens hurt my ears, too," Buster said. "But that's no reason to panic. If you'd broken the window with the ball, you'd be in big trouble. Especially after you dug out of the

1

yard two feeding times ago."

"You're right," I sighed, touching my nose to his. "I'll be more careful next time I hear a siren."

"You should be more careful in general," he retorted poking his head into the hole. "When did you dig this?"

"Earlier. While you were napping." Sliding back onto the lawn, I shook until the star tag on my collar rattled.

He scrambled after me. "Why? Darcy will be furious."

I looked at his black wavy coat gleaming in the sun. "Come on, Darcy won't see the hole. It's under the branches."

He lowered his floppy ears and tucked his long tail between his legs. "If you keep digging up the yard, her parents will get mad and find a new home for you."

"She won't let them," I scoffed, tossing my head and pointing my tail to the sky.

"She won't have anything to say about it." He nudged my shoulder. "Let's find something else to do. You wanna play I'm a cow and you're a herding dog?"

I almost laughed. We were both about grown, but he stood taller than me. With imagination, I could turn him into a cow and chase him. "I'm tired of that game. I want a real cow to herd, if I'm going to herd. Let's make up something new. How about jumping off the porch?"

"The porch?" He glanced at the human den where Darcy and her parents, Margaret and Bob lived.

"Sure." I wagged my tail. "How could we get in trouble doing that? We'll land in the middle of the lawn."

He thought a moment. "That's true. Okay, race you over there."

We charged away from the bushes and flew across the grass. As the breeze ruffled my pointy ears, I rollicked and frolicked. I loved running best in the world. When Darcy and I did it together, I was in dog heaven. It almost made long days here in the yard worthwhile, even though I had nothing to do until she came home from school or karate or soccer practice.

The breath tore in my lungs as I dashed. Not far from the porch, a stone grill loomed, filling me with the smell of cooked chicken, beef, and pork. Closer and closer I came, pretending it was a cow.

"Belle," Buster barked. "You'll crack your head."

Cutting tight corners was my second favorite game. Running as hard as I could, I dropped my belly close to the ground. Almost touching the grill, I made a tight half circle around it, and dashed to the porch, clearing the steps with a bound.

Buster gallumpfed behind me, long legs swinging, tongue lolling. He scrambled up the steps, panting. "Dog biscuits, Belle. Sometimes I think you have fleas in your brain."

With a wag of my tail, I let out a woof. "I'm a herding dog, Buster. I know how to dodge stuff. It's fun."

He caught his breath. "If you say so. Who's going to jump first?"

I pranced to the human den door, turned, and raced toward the edge of the porch. Springing, I landed inches from the fire pit under the grill. The spot had the smell of charred wood.

What a perfect landing. Heart pounding, I dashed back to the porch. "Your turn Buster."

He lumbered to the door, his movements reminding me of a bear I once saw in a field.

Turning, he made a lolloping run and jumped, sailing across the grass toward the grill.

I held my breath. He could spring farther than I could, but couldn't turn as fast when he landed. Would he hit the ground in time to dodge the grill?

Buster landed in front of the grill and slid into the fire pit. Ash spewed into the air and drifted toward the porch. His head smacked the meat grate. The grate flew upward then bounced into the grass.

Holy bones. I bounded to him. "Are you all right?"

He pulled his front legs out of the ashes and stood.

Catching his breath, he shook dust out of his fur. "I'm fine. We retriever types should swim, not jump, I guess."

Lowering my ears, I looked at ashes scattered on the ground. "We'll be in for it, now."

"I'll be in for it, you mean," he retorted, wiping his face in the grass. "They'll never know it was *your* idea to jump off the porch. *My* name will be Mutt when they see the grill, and me all full of stuff."

"You could have jumped in another direction, Buster." I growled.

"I should have said 'no' to your dumb game," he retorted, drawing back his lips. "You're always getting us in trouble. I shouldn't listen to you."

My tail dropped between my legs. "I know. I'm sorry. I'm not used to being a house pet. I grew up in a barn, remember?"

"I do," he sighed. "All right, we're both at fault, but I'll be the one punished. You watch." Flopping down, he rubbed his legs into the lawn.

When he stood up, I touched my nose to his. "You'll get rid of the ashes by the time they all come home. They'll think the wind knocked the grate off the grill."

He glanced at trees swaying beyond our fence, then at his paws. "They're a little cleaner, I guess. I suppose we might get out of this one. And if not, there's nothin' we can do about it now." With a final shake, he ran his tongue over his chops. "Come on. Let's find something else to play. It's too nice a day to argue."

Good ole Buster. Things never bothered him for long. I spotted the grill's cooking rack near my feet. "Hey, there's lamb here." I grabbed a charred tidbit. "Have some. It's good."

He dropped his nose next to mine. Tongues slapping, we gnawed and slurped the rack clean.

"Now what," I asked, running my tongue over my chops. "Should we dig out and go explore the neighbor-hood?" I glanced at the fence ringing the yard. "We can make that hole I started bigger until it goes under the fence."

Buster sighed. "Belle, where do you come up with such flea brained ideas?"

"I was a wild dog before I came to live here, remember?" I trotted back to the shrubs and ducked under the branches.

"Belle," He pleaded, sliding in beside me. "I know it's dull around here when Darcy's gone but..."

Dirt flew under my feet as I pushed deep into the ground. "Come on, Buster. If we do this right, we'll be back before Darcy knows we're gone."

He skittered backwards, shaking until his tags rattled. "Don't you like being her pet?"

"It was fun in the summer when Darcy or her mom or dad were home to play with us." I kept digging. "But now it's awful. I'm used to taking care of myself, thinking to stay alive. I don't know what to do all day."

"You can play with me."

I looked at his sweet black Labrador retriever face. Irish Setter curls covered his neck and chest. "Buster, you're the best friend a dog could have, but I want more than just to play all the time."

"Belle, living with Darcy has gotta be better than living with Bonehead and Toby. Those guys might have killed you. You're lucky Darcy found you when they dumped you out of their truck. Why can't you put up with just being lazy sometimes?"

I shuddered remembering the moment Big Toby, Bonehead's son, chased me across the place where people buy the stinky water to make their cars go. Big Toby's sour stench had choked me as he stomped on my tail. Darcy had been sitting in her aunt's car that was getting its special water. Darcy had grabbed me away from Big Toby.

Still, I scattered more dirt. "Bonehead and Big Toby were dangerous, but holy bones when they weren't bothering me, I sure chased a lot of rabbits."

"You remember the fun parts of being loose. What about kicks in the ribs, shivering in a barn on a cold night, and eating rotten meat? When you first got here, you had some stories about that, too."

I snorted. Buster was right. Life on the loose wasn't always fun. When Darcy found me, I'd been a filthy mess, full of fleas. I didn't trust or love anybody. Now I couldn't imagine life without Darcy.

I loved how she stroked me good night before I settled on the rug at the foot of her bed. Licking her awake in the morning and standing by her closet while she chose her school clothes was a blast. In Maryville Park when she wore those wheeled shoes she called skates, I ran hard to beat her to the lake.

I'd even gone to obedience school for her, and learned to sit, come, stay, and lie down. Buster and I both got a paper called a Canine Good Citizen Certificate. I had no idea what it meant, but it sure made Darcy proud. So I was proud, too.

Today I knew nobody would give me a certificate like that, but who cared? I wanted to get out and run, to meet up with something and think my way through it, without anybody to tell me how, like I used to before I became a pet.

I kept digging. "I'll just go around the block, and come back."

Lifting his tail and curling it over his back, Buster looked down his nose at me. "Belle, you're being selfish."

"What are you talking about?" I stopped digging. "Didn't I play fetch with you this morning until you decided to go to sleep? Didn't I share the stuff off the grill?"

"Yes. But you're doing other stupid things. You kept messing with the waste baskets in the human den, so now we can't use the doggie door when nobody's home."

I tucked my tail between my legs. "Yeah, maybe I shouldn't have done that, but I found good bones for us."

Buster half smiled. "Yes, and that was fun. But I'd like to get in the house for a drink of water. I'm tired of leaves falling into my bowl."

Guilt pricked me. Waste baskets were loaded with wonderful stuff, but Buster shouldn't have to suffer for my interest in them. "All right, I'll leave the garbage alone, I promise. Just don't act upset and tip them off when I roam once in a while, okay? I have to do it."

Buster sighed. "Sometimes, I feel like roaming, too. You got a deal. I'll play dumb."

"Thanks." Licking his face I stuck my head into the hole. "A little more work and we're out of here." My nostrils flared. "Oh, squirrel. Smell!"

He sniffed. "You'll never catch that old toughie. He's too smart. You want to chase squirrels, wait until we go visit Darcy's aunt and uncle."

"I want to chase them now," I growled, burrowing deeper under the fence. "Maybe one day I'll catch one. Then we can have a feast." Breathing deep, I smelled the aroma of the world beyond the fence: drying leaves, other dogs, cats, chipmunks, birds, garbage cans full of meat, the creek that flowed from town to the lake at the park.

My nose lingered on the stream smell. "Hey, Buster, you know what? I'll just go visit Darcy's Aunt Ellen now. Her human den isn't far away, and I know how to get there. I'll chase a few squirrels and come back. In fact, why don't you come along and jump in the creek? That'll wash off the last of the ashes.

"Belle, we'll be caught for sure, if Aunt Ellen sees us," Buster protested.

"She won't if we stay along the creek in the woods."

"We shouldn't," Buster sighed. "We're in enough trouble already."

"My fur is getting thick," I answered returning to my digging. "The cold time is coming. There won't be many more chances to swim before it gets here."

"You're right." He glanced up through the bushes to the

sky. "But Darcy will be coming soon. The sun is more than half way to its disappearing place." He wiggled his nose. "But I smell turtles. Now that's something to catch and eat."

"No thanks. The only turtle I ever ate made me barf in Darcy's sleeping burrow. Come on." I dug faster."A dip and a turtle for you, and a chase for me."

Buster licked his chops. "All right. I could use a snack that isn't a dog biscuit." Scrunching down next to me, he extended his paws. "Let me help with that hole."

We dug and dug, the smell of life outside the fence spurring us on. I could picture the squirrels in the woods behind Aunt Ellen's human den. Then my nose caught another odor, sweet with the stuff humans call powder yet spicy with sweat. Raising my head, I sniffed.

Darcy's smell after a day in school and soccer or karate practice. Was she home? Maybe we'd better back out of this escape and look innocent. I paused. "Buster, wait."

"What?" He touched his nose to mine. "What's wrong, you getting cold paws?"

"Maybe." I let my nostrils wiggle. "Do you smell Darcy?"

He sniffed. "No."

I poked my nose out of the brush in the direction of the human den and smelled harder. The odor of pine needles, damp earth, and worms filled my nostrils, but not her scent.

"I don't smell her," said Buster." Squeeze through the hole, and let's go before it's too late." Flattening himself, he wriggled under the fence.

Well, maybe she walked by the bushes a while ago and her smell lingered.

Dropping onto my belly, I followed Buster, focusing on the aroma of squirrels to hide the guilt that swelled in me.

Chapter 2

A Nasty Surprise

"What in dog heaven is this, Buster?" We stood in the trees by the creek staring up the grassy slope to Aunt Ellen's human den. An empty run with bowls and a dog house stood near the den. The dog who usually hung out there, Painter, was racing across the lawn on a very short leash. A sturdy boy ran beside him.

9

Ears cocked, and short tail straight behind, Painter sprang over tiny fences scattered across the grass. His brown, gray, and yellow spots rippled in his white coat as he leapt and dove.

"That kid's teaching him to jump. Like Darcy taught you to jump through her hula hoop," Buster replied. "Painter looks like he's having a good time."

My nose flared, catching a familiar scent. "The boy! That's Big Toby, Bonehead's kid. I'm sure of it."

Buster settled in a leaf pile." He can't be Big Toby. Big Toby was fat and stank like a pukey stomach. Or like he was scared of the world. This kid doesn't smell bad, and he's thinner than Toby was."

Buster had fleas in his brain. Big Toby stank like barf all right, but he wasn't scared of anything, especially defenseless dogs.

Painter knocked something apart that looked like a fence. The boy stopped running and jerked Painter hard.

"Wrong! No! Bad dog!"

Painter tucked his tail between his legs.

"That's Toby's voice," I growled. "I'd know it any-where."

The boy pushed dark hair out of his face and put the fence together. Then taking the leash he led Painter toward the house, turned, and ran toward us.

"Jump."

Painter cleared the fence.

The boy tossed him a treat. "Good dog."

I sniffed hard. The kid smelled like spicy sweat, but he had a touch of a sour peppery odor that I knew too well. "That *is* Big Toby," I growled. "Take a good sniff."

Buster wiggled his nose. "You're right."

"He's mad at Painter." My growl turned to a snarl.

"No wait, Belle," Buster said. "Something's changed about him. Anyway why do you suppose he's here at Aunt Ellen's?"

"I don't think we want to know." I ran to follow the

creek back home. "He might hurt us, especially me."

Buster let his tongue dangle. "He doesn't seem to be hurting Painter. And maybe Painter deserved to get yelled at. Maybe he wasn't paying attention to what he was doing."

Painter dove into what looked like a huge dead snake. I held my breath.

Toby ran to the other end of the snake, clapping his hands. Painter bounced out tail flying, and slurped the boy's face.

Buster smiled. "Looks like both of them are having more fun than chasing a million squirrels."

Fleas had definitely invaded Buster's brain. "How can you be so calm? Toby bounced a rock of your head last summer. Let's get out of here before he does it again."

Sighing, Buster rose and faced the creek." All right, but at least let me grab a turtle first."

"Hurry and don't get too wet, or we'll be busted for sure. Stay in the shadows." Hunkering down, I watched Big Toby and Painter.

Painter jumped over long things, leaped through round ones, and ran between tall skinny stuff. He walked in a high place and raced up a long board that sloped toward the sky. As he passed the middle, the other end of the board tilted to the ground. Painter strolled off.

"Good boy." Toby patted him.

The sound of a splash and the smell of Buster's wet fur reached me. Holy dog biscuits, he was swimming. Even if we got home unnoticed, Darcy would take one glance at him and knew we'd been out.

Twisting my head, I gave him a dark look, but he stood with his back to me.

I faced the yard again, just in time for two new odors to greet my nose. One smelled like flowers in a summer garden. The other was spicy and musky, with a touch of cat nip in it. Aunt Ellen and Misty. I looked up at the human den. Aunt Ellen stepped out, a white cat behind her.

I shrank deeper into the shadows. I liked Aunt Ellen, but no sense in letting her or the cat see me. I didn't want to get into trouble any sooner than I had to.

"Okay Toby, it's time to stop," Aunt Ellen called. Soft blond hair blew around her heart-shaped face. I was too far away to see her eyes but I knew they were like the blue sky on a summer morning.

Taking the short leash off Painter, Toby gave him a pat and looked at Aunt Ellen. "Okay, ma'am. I'm hungry. Got any grapes?"

Grapes? When I lived with him, Big Toby stuffed himself on junk food and sodas until he got sick. Then he kicked me. What was going on here?

"We have some fruit and some carrots." Aunt Ellen walked onto the grass. "By the way, what are you supposed to say when Painter doesn't do something right? Is it 'no, bad dog'?"

Big Toby looked at the ground. "No, ma'am. I guess I should say 'wrong,' and make him do it again."

Ma'am? I stared at Big Toby's back as he jogged into the human den. People said ma'am to be polite. Last I'd heard from him, he'd called Darcy something that sounded like sitch or witch. No way had he learned to be polite. Any minute he'd try to kick Aunt Ellen.

Painter trotted to his run, stuck his muzzle in a water bowl and gulped.

Fur ruffling in the breeze, Misty sauntered across the lawn and rubbed her fluffy back on fence that Painter had jumped. Then she strolled up the slope to the high place, walked, and sprang off.

"Look out!" I yelped. "You'll hurt yourself."

She landed on her feet.

My cry turned to a snort. Typical cat. If she jumped off the moon she'd land on her feet. I'd break my legs jumping like she did.

Misty looked up.

Uh-oh. I tried to scrunch into the tangle of tree trunks.

"Belle," she mewed and streaked toward me. "What are you doing here? Are Buster and Darcy with you?"

"Darcy isn't." I glanced at the creek where Buster wallowed. "What's going on?"

"Ask Painter. That stuff on the lawn is his." Misty batted leaves into the air. "Well, aren't you glad to see me?"

Again, how like a cat. They'd never say they were happy to see you.

Spotting Misty, Buster scrambled onto the bank and shook.

She danced away from the droplets. "Cut it out."

Buster let his tongue loll and came to lie down beside me.

Arching her back, Misty narrowed her eyes at him.

"What is Big Toby doing in Ellen's den, Misty?" I laid my ears flat on my head.

"Living here. He's something called a foster child. I guess Ellen found out she couldn't have kids, so being the Sweet Mama she is, she and Jim took Toby in. I'll never know why. She was pretty mad at him when he tried to hurt us last summer."

Ellen couldn't have kids? I'd give her an extra nuzzle when I saw her. My Mama had loved me and my brothers and sisters when I was a pup on Bonehead's farm. Ellen probably would have loved her kids the same way. But she had fleas in her brain to take someone as mean as Big Toby. I looked at Misty. "How can anybody stand him?"

She licked a paw. "I spit at him or bite. He's learned how much teasing I'll take."

Cats took care of themselves. "Sometime it's lucky we understand more people talk that they know we do," I said.

"Toby really likes Painter." She glanced at the lawn. "And that's fine, because you couldn't get me to hop through hoops and over jumps like those on the grass."

What about Painter? Did he like Toby?

"You seem to like that high place where you jumped a minute ago, Misty."

She nodded at the high place. "That's a dog walk. It's cool. I like to jump off the teeter-totter, too." She pointed her chin at the board that fell when Painter stood in the middle of it. "I let Painter chase me on both."

She twitched her tail and looked up at the dog run. "Hey Painter. Belle's here. Come down and explain all your junk to her."

Painter raised his head, water dripping down his chin whiskers. "Well, long time no woof." He romped over to me. "What are you doing?"

His coat bounced with wiry curls. Brown eyes sparkling, he cocked his head.

"You're lookin' good, Fox Face. But you're here without Darcy, huh?"

"You got it." Judging from the sun, she'd be back at her human den by now. We'd missed our chance to sneak back into the yard.

Buster glanced at the lawn. "What's Toby making you do, Painter?"

I nuzzled Painter, searching for the smell of bloody cuts. "Is he hurting you?"

"No. He gets impatient with me sometimes, but he's better than he was when he first came here. We're doing dog agility for something he calls 4-H."

"What?" Buster and I barked together.

"Dog agility. It's where you run on a path and do tricks like jump over jumps. Fastest dog wins a prize for his human."

A prize. When I lived with Big Toby he screamed and yelled when he played a game for a prize and didn't win it. Poor Painter. Toby must be beating him into being the best. I took another sniff of his coat. It smelled clean and healthy.

"You like dog agility?" Buster asked.

"Sure it's fun, especially the part where you go through tunnels." He glanced at the thing that reminded me of a snake. "Of course, that's a natural for me 'cuz I'm a terrier. We like to dig into small places. You want to try it?"

"You mean run for a prize?" I tucked my tail between my legs. "I don't think so."

"No, just play on the equipment. Ellen and Toby won't mind." Painter licked his lips. "Holy dog biscuits, he sure changed since he beat us all up last summer. He went to some kind of place called boot camp for tough kids." He shook his head. "The people there didn't take any nonsense off him. Aunt Ellen and Uncle Jim won't either."

"I'll bet Toby and Uncle Jim hate each other." Toby ran wild on Bonehead's farm. Uncle Jim expected good behavior from everyone.

"Toby likes Uncle Jim," Painter said.

"Don't ask me why." Swishing her tail, Misty studied her front paws.

Uncle Jim asked an animal doctor to declaw Misty when she was a kitten. Once Uncle Jim stepped on me, and I bit him. He'd been ready to whisk me to the dog pound until Aunt Ellen stopped him.

"I can't imagine Toby liking Uncle Jim."

Painter wagged his tail. "He's not that bad. Remember he didn't have pets until he married Aunt Ellen. He doesn't quite know what to do with us." Painter licked my nose. "So you want to try the agility course?"

"Can you do it without Toby?" I looked at the teeter-totter.

"I don't know why not. It's easy."

Buster stood up. "Let's do it. I'm curious."

Why not? I liked jumping through the hula hoop. I might like leaping fences and burrowing through tunnels, too.

Painter led us up the lawn. A few dog lengths from the thing Misty had called a jump, he broke into a run. Buster and I tore after him. Painter cleared the bar. Buster got ahead of me with his long legs, lobbed himself into the air and landed with a thud. I sprang over it easily and touched down with hardly a sound.

Painter headed toward a big hoop hanging from a tree. "Let's try the tire jump."

The others sailed through ahead of me. As I flung myself upward, my heart thumped and the wind ruffled my fur. This was as much fun as running when Darcy wore her wheeled shoes.

At the next jump, my foot touched the bar and I knocked it down. It didn't hurt me when it fell, and I kept running.

Painter dived into the snake tunnel. I shot after him, stumbled on the tunnel's slippery floor, and half staggered and half clawed my way out. Buster wallowed half way through and struggled out, sneezing. He was big and strong but not light on his feet.

"Come chase me." Misty danced in front of Painter.

With a playful growl he lunged. She mock hissed and scurried up the long wooden slope to the high place she had called the dog walk. Painter bolted after her. I streaked behind him, and Buster lumbered last.

Misty cheated and jumped off the walk.

Painter led us down the slope at the other end.

Misty met us at the bottom. "I dare you to chase me on the teeter-totter." She batted her green eyes at the board that pointed into the air.

"Double dare," Painter barked.

She scrambled toward the sky. We followed. The wooden slope jerked.

Buster skidded behind me.

"Hang on Belle," he panted.

I tried to brace my legs. Painter stopped. I bumped his hips. Buster hit my butt. The teeter-totter swayed. I struggled to stay on my feet, scratching, trying to dig my claws into the board. My paws skidded. Fear grabbed my stomach. I was going to fall.

Darcy's voice reached my ears. "Belle, stay. Don't move."

Her spicy sweet after school smell wafted to me. The sweaty sick stench of fear and the pepper of anger mixed with it.

Somehow, she'd found us. She'd get me off this thing. Twisting sideways, I tried to see her, but could not.

Misty shot into the air like a flying lion. The teeter-totter whooshed down.

I thought my stomach would fall out. The teeter-totter slammed into the earth. My nose smacked Painter's tail. Buster's face walloped my flank. The force sent one of my back feet skidding over the teeter-totter's edge. My front leg followed.

Buster jumped, landing on all fours. I tumbled sideways and hit the ground landing on my shoulder. I yipped in pain.

Chapter 3

A Big Mess

"Belle." Darcy knelt beside me in the bright outer fur she wore for soccer practice. "What were you doing up there?"

A swarm of angry bees seemed to buzz through my head. My shoulder burned. I couldn't move.

She skittered away from me and tapped the grass. "Belle, come. Are you all right? Can you walk?" A smell like sweat on a sick person came from her. *Fear.*

The door of the human den opened. Aunt Ellen and

Toby burst out.

"What on earth!" Aunt Ellen exclaimed.

My head cleared. The bees turned into a motor roaring near the creek. Maybe one of those things people called a lawn mower. I tottered to my feet and swayed.

"Come, Belle." Darcy coaxed.

I took a cautious step. My shoulder ached, but I managed to creep to her.

Her fear smell grew fainter. She took hold of my scruff. "Belle, now that I know you're all right, I wonder if I should hug you or be mad at you."

I tucked my tail between my legs and glanced up at Buster.

His head dropped until his nose almost touched the ground. "Here it comes," he said in a rumble only I could hear.

Darcy looked at Aunt Ellen, who now stood beside her.

"These guys should be called Houdini One and Two. Lucky I saw them get out as I was coming home." She grabbed Buster's collar. "Bad dogs."

I *had* smelled her just as we were leaving our yard.

Buster touched my ear. "We should have trusted your nose."

"Why did they go up the teeter-totter?" Aunt Ellen looked bewildered.

Giving her an innocent look, Misty washed her whiskers.

I growled.

"Belle," said Darcy.

She was right. This wasn't Misty's fault. We accepted her dare to run up the teeter-totter. A bump on the shoulder was my own doing

Toby trotted up. A milk mustache encircled his thick lips. "Holy c-." He muttered around a mouth full of fruit.

Aunt Ellen stared at him, unsmiling.

He swallowed. "Holy cow. Is Belle all right? She ain't..." He glanced at Aunt Ellen. "She isn't hurt, is she?"

"She's fine." Darcy glared at him. "Why weren't you out here with your agility equipment, Toby Johnson. If the 4-H Pooch Patrol knew you'd left it unattended they'd have your head."

"Oh, come on, Darcy," Toby retorted. "You're not even in 4-H, and you've never done agility with a dog. What do you know about it?"

"I'm a junior volunteer at the Animal League." She hung on to me and Buster. A peppery angry smell had replaced the odor of fear. "We learned that dogs can get hurt on agility equipment."

Aunt Ellen stepped between them. "Calm down, Darcy. I called Toby inside." She turned to him. "We should have brought your snack out. You could have put your equipment away while you ate."

Toby scuffed his foot on the ground. "I didn't think about it, ma'am."

"You've probably never thought about anything in your life, except food," Darcy muttered under her breath.

"What?" asked Aunt Ellen.

"Nothing, never mind," she said. "I'd better take the dogs home."

"Just a minute." Aunt Ellen put her hands on her hips. A pepper smell rose from her skin and she locked her gaze on Darcy's, then Toby's. "I'm disappointed in both of you," Aunt Ellen said.

Holy bones, why was she mad at Darcy? Toby deserved what Darcy said. I thrust my nose into Darcy's hand.

Toby looked at the ground. He smelled afraid.

Darcy grimaced. Her angry smell lessened. The sour odor of guilt replaced it.

Darcy drew a deep breath and controlled herself. "Okay, I'm sorry I got mad," she said to Toby. "It wasn't right. Going inside and leaving the equipment wasn't totally your doing."

Aunt Ellen shifted her gaze to him.

He scuffed his shoe in the dirt. "Uh...I said some stuff,

too. Sorry."

Painter touched my nose. "I guess we shouldn't be alone on agility equipment. Part of what happened is my fault and Misty's."

Her tail twitched. "You didn't have to take my dare."

"You didn't have to offer it." Buster stared her down. "I think we're all a lot smarter than we've been behaving today."

"That's for sure," I said. "If I'd stayed in the yard, this whole mess would never have happened."

Misty pounced on a leaf. "Okay."

Aunt Ellen took a step back. "All right. Darcy would you like to try Belle on the agility course?"

"I need to get home, Aunt Ellen." Darcy fidgeted, stepping away from Toby.

"I'll call your mother and tell her where you are." Aunt Ellen didn't move.

Darcy looked down. For a minute her peppery anger smell came again.

Aunt Ellen folded her arms.

Darcy sighed and nodded.

Aunt Ellen looked at Toby. "Would you please show her what to do?"

"Yes, ma'am." He pulled the short leash from his pocket and held it up for Darcy to see. "This is a tab. You hook it on the dog's collar and then just lead her through the course."

"What if a dog doesn't know what to do?" Darcy pushed her hair out of her eyes.

"You steer her through it, like you're teaching a trick." He held out the tab. "Try it."

Aunt Ellen went back into the human den. In a moment, I heard her clattering in the burrow where she kept the people food.

Darcy looked at Buster.

He lay down with a burp that smelled like turtles. "No thanks. I've run enough for today," he said with his eyes.

21

She turned to me. My shoulder didn't hurt anymore, so might as well help out.

Darcy snapped the tab on me. It was so short; she had to bend to hang onto it. We trotted to the first jump. "Over," she commanded.

I jumped and she led me to the tire. Springing through was okay, but not quite as much fun as when I jumped through the hula hoop.

She released me at the tunnel entrance. I clawed through and she caught the tab. Meeting her brought some excitement back. I pranced across the dog walk, ears and tail straight up.

Aunt Ellen stuck her head out the food burrow window. "She looks good up there with those white feet. I'd bet she'd make a good agility dog."

I lifted my head high as I stepped back to the grass. She always said my black muzzle, gold fur, and foxy face set me apart from the pack. Now my feet made me look good, too. I looked around the yard to see how else I could show off.

Darcy zigzagged me around some tall thin twig things that stood in a row like saplings. I sensed I should make tight corners around them, but with her pulling me on the tab it was hard.

"Tell her to weave," Toby called. "Those are weave poles."

Darcy said nothing.

Aunt Ellen cleared her throat.

"In 4-H they said those take a year for a dog to learn," said Toby.

Spinning away from the last pole, I caught my breath and tried to veer toward another jump. These were the most fun thing on the course. Darcy guided me toward the teeter-totter.

Not for a whole box of dog biscuits. I dug my claws into the grass.

Toby jogged over. "Put the teeter down and let her walk

from the middle to the ground."

Not even for the biggest bone in the world. Lowering my head and twisting my neck, I slid my head out of my collar, and shot away from them toward the creek.

Darcy sprinted after me. Nostrils flaring, I sprang out of her reach. A peppery, barfy stench hit my nose. So did rotten fruit smell of the strange water people drank that made them crazy – made them beat dogs.

Bonehead! Toby's dad. He must be in the woods by the creek. If he came out, he and Toby would hurt all of us. I knew hanging around here wasn't a good idea. Baring my teeth and glaring at the trees, I built a snarl into a gigantic bark.

Darcy closed her fingers on my scruff. "Stop it, Belle."

Pushing her behind me, I bellowed. "Buster! Painter! Smell! Trouble!"

They flew down the lawn, noses wide. "Bonehead! Get him," I woofed.

Misty raced behind them and scrambled up a tree.

The bushes rustled. Bonehead's odor began to fade. He must be running away. Buster and Painter churned into the creek. Foam spurted. Wrenching free of Darcy, I bolted after them, though I hated water plastering down my thick fur.

Why in dog heaven was Bonehead here? He should be in jail. Could he have escaped? Was that why the sirens earlier nearly ruptured my ears?

I caught a whiff of the water people used to make cars go. Bonehead's stench mixed with it. A motor sputtered. Both odors moved away fast.

Darcy ran to the creek bank. "Belle, come here. Some idiot's just four wheeling back there, that's all."

Butting her thigh with my nose, I tried to herd her back up the hill. We needed to go home, now. I didn't care what punishment awaited me.

"Cut it out Belle," She slipped my collar over my head and turned to find Aunt Ellen and Toby at her elbow.

"Did you get a look at who it was?" Aunt Ellen frowned.

Darcy shook her head.

"Always someone to ruin a nice little walking path," Aunt Ellen sighed. "Maybe Jim needs to build some kind of barrier for us to keep jerks away."

If she only knew which jerk she was talking about.

The cell phone on her belt rang. She glanced at it, arched her brows and hurried away from us before she answered.

Painter and Buster touched my nose. Painter spoke in a voice that only dogs can hear. "Only time she scurries like that when the phone rings is when she doesn't want Toby to hear something."

I thought about the sirens we heard. "What if Bonehead got out of jail and someone's calling to let Aunt Ellen and Uncle Jim know?"

Scrambling down the tree trunk, Misty joined us. "Let me run after Ellen and see what I can hear." She hurried toward the human den, arriving just as Aunt Ellen opened the door to go in.

I shivered. "Wonder how long Bonehead was out there. I didn't smell him when we got here, did you Buster?"

"No." Lowering his ears he thought. "And I didn't hear anything like a motor pull up and stop, did you?"

I cocked my head. "Yes! When I fell off the teeter totter, I thought something was buzzing but when my head cleared, it was a motor. I thought maybe someone was cutting a lawn on the other side of the creek.

"Maybe we were all concentrating on what happened to you and didn't hear it," suggested Painter.

I pressed closer to Darcy, trying to make her move. Didn't she realize what had just happened?

She started up the lawn, holding my collar. Toby followed.

"On TV the dogs run agility courses without a leash, don't they?" She spoke without turning around.

Holy bones, she doesn't know what happened. What about

Toby? Did he know his dad was there? Was he planning to meet up with him and start torturing animals again?

"The best dogs do run agility courses without a leash," Toby answered. "I want to do it with the 4-H Pooch Patrol at the County Fair in July."

Was he as unaware of Bonehead as Darcy? Or was he lying?

Darcy glanced over her shoulder and laughed. "Do you really think you can get Painter to obey you off a leash?"

He stuck out his chin. "I'm gonna – going to – try."

Neither one of them seemed to care about Bonehead. There wasn't much more I could do to warn them. With a sigh, I put my nose against Painter's ear. "Can *you* do agility without a leash?"

"If Toby points me in the direction I need to go, I can do parts of it."

"What's it like?"

"You're running free except you're in close touch with your human."

The door to the human den opened. Aunt Ellen stepped out, Misty prancing after her.

"Toby, I need you to put the agility equipment away." Auntie Ellen said. "Then come inside."

Buster, Painter, and I looked at each other then at Misty.

"She was talking to the people who help her when Toby has a problem. Bonehead managed to escape from the police when they were transferring him to another jail. They're going to tell Toby tonight, and decide if he should stay here or if he should move."

I almost felt sorry for him, but I also hoped he'd go away, so Bonehead could follow him somewhere else.

Darcy looked at Aunt Ellen. "Thanks for letting me try agility with Belle. We need to do something to get her focused and settled down. Maybe agility is a good idea."

Holy bones. I'd forgotten the trouble that was coming when I got home. I lowered my ears and my tail.

"Discipline could calm her down," Aunt Ellen replied.

Discipline? That meant punishment. Oh dog biscuits, I was in for it.

Darcy looked at me. "Maybe we can talk mom into letting you try it. I'd sure hate to lose you, but she's about ready to give you away." She began to smell like leaves decaying in a pond. *Sad.*

I nuzzled her. *You won't let that happen. You can't. Especially now with Bonehead loose.* If he tried to take Toby away, would he take me, too?

But I knew if Darcy's mom chose to get rid of me, Darcy could do nothing about it. Cuddling close to Darcy, I whimpered.

Chapter 4

Life: Complete Confusion

"Can't we try dog agility with her?" Kneeling beside me, Darcy rubbed my ears. "I understand she can't keep running away, but she's so sweet." Her voice broke.

I sat on the floor in the food burrow at the edge of the human eating table, my head on her knee. Her parents sat on chairs. Buster looked in from the porch, wet fur plastered to his ribs and shoulders.

"Belle's an active little dog, honey," Bob said, reaching down and scratched my back. "Don't you think she might need somebody who's home all day to work with her on something like that?"

I looked up into Bob's brown eyes. Glancing back tenderly, he stroked me with a big hand.

"What about Buster?" Darcy wiped a tear from her cheek.

I looked through the door at him and shivered. Would they send both of us away? If they split us up, and he went to a horrible home, it would be my fault.

Margaret glanced at him. "He seems happy romping in the back yard," she mused. "Until Belle stirs him up. I doubt she's big enough to knock the grate off a grill, but I bet she was chasing him when he did it."

I looked up at her. She was tall and slim, like Darcy would one day be, and had the same fluffy golden hair and azure blue eyes.

She patted my nose. "Belle, what are we going to do with you?"

With a tiny tail wag, I gave her fingers a dog kiss. Buster would probably stay here and be safe. They'd get rid of my flea bitten influence on him.

Once they decided to give me away, what should I do? Dig out of the back yard a final time and hit the road? Or let them find a home for me and try to be someone else's pet?

How could I be anybody else's pet but Darcy's? How could I lie at the foot of any bed but hers? I whimpered and nuzzled her. Dog biscuits, I'd miss that tender flowery scent of hers, if I had to go. My whine became a small howl.

Darcy caressed my shoulder. "It's almost like she knows what we're talking about, Mom."

"Scientists are beginning to find out some animals have very sophisticated communication systems," Bob looked down at me. "Darn it, Belle, we all like you. Why do you have to be such a scalawag?"

"Because she's bored, Bob." With a glance at him, Margaret gave me another pat. "Dogs were bred to do jobs. Belle needs one. Maybe we should find a farmer to take her."

Margaret understood. She helped kids in school who had trouble.

"Oh, no. Couldn't we just try agility first?" Sniffing Darcy reached onto the table, grabbed a paper napkin, and blew her nose. "She's so smart. I know she could do agility. Please, Mom? Please, Dad?"

Margaret hugged her shoulders. "Some dogs just aren't house pets. Belle survived on her own for a good chunk of her life. That's going to affect her behavior."

"But you're a psychologist. You must be able to do something. Couldn't you try?"

Buster pawed the door and whined. "Belle, find some way to convince them to keep you."

I ran and pressed my nose to the screen. "I'm sorry. I've been really stupid."

His ears and tail hung low.

Darcy held back sobs. "I'll miss the way she nips my heels in the morning. And the way she runs right up to something and weaves around it..." She stopped.

Bob and Margaret looked at her, then at us.

"Buster and Belle adore each other," Margaret murmured.

"H-how c-could you separate them?" Tears rolled down Darcy's cheeks.

"Maybe I could reinforce the fence," Bob mused. "After all, we aren't the only people in the world with dogs that escape the yard."

"No, I suppose we're not," Margaret agreed.

Darcy caught her breath and wiped her face with the back of her hand. "Belle likes to weave around stuff. Shepherd dogs do that. You do weaving in dog agility. She'd be perfect at it."

Margaret turned to her. "She's certainly well behaved in a lot of ways. She got the top mark in her Canine Good Citizen class, didn't she?"

"Yes. When she's busy, she's fine." Darcy's gaze cleared. "What if we got her into dog agility? Couldn't we at least try? Mom? Dad? Please?" She stretched out the word.

I turned from Buster and watched Darcy and Margaret.

Darcy counted on her fingers. "Agility's full of the stuff Belle does best: making tight circles, sliding through small spaces, dodging obstacles."

"I suppose it's a possibility," Margaret nodded. "It would burn off some of her extra energy for sure."

She had that right. I was beat after all the digging, running and jumping this afternoon. Yawning big, I trotted back to Darcy and lay down at her feet.

"She's trying to show us how pooped she is," Bob laughed.

Darcy and Margaret chuckled with him.

Then Margaret sobered. "But Darcy, you'd have to work with her every day. Could you manage that and soccer, plus karate *and* your homework, now that you've joined the choir and don't have study hall?" Leaning down, she pushed strands of Darcy's hair out of her eyes. "You're barely going to get your assignments done tonight before you have to go to bed."

I held my breath and glanced at Buster. Ears cocked, he waited with me.

Darcy nodded. "I know I can do it. I promise, Mom."

"Don't take on more than you can handle," Margaret said.

"Sometimes you don't know your limit until you reach it," Bob suggested.

Darcy grinned at him. "Or what you really want to do until you try."

"True," answered Margaret. She turned to Darcy. "But where can you do agility? Our back yard isn't big enough for a lot of equipment."

"There's an agility club in town with a Junior Handler's Program." Darcy rubbed my belly. "I've seen their notices at the animal shelter. They're always looking for members."

"They meet way out in the country," said Bob. "Between your mother's work schedule and mine, it would be impossible to get you out there to practice."

"And Aunt Ellen couldn't do it any more, now that Toby's at their house." Darcy sighed. "I miss her and Uncle Jim coming to all my games."

Margaret gave her a sharp glance. "She still comes fairly often, doesn't she?"

"Yes," Darcy admitted.

"How about doing 4-H agility," Bob asked. "You could walk to Aunt Ellen's and practice on the equipment they've set up for Toby. I'm sure they'd let you."

I shuddered. Why couldn't I speak People Language at times like these?

Darcy's mouth twisted like she'd bit into something sour, and she drew her arms close to her body. "No way am I going to practice anything with Toby Johnson."

Recalling how he treated Painter when the jump fell, I pressed my nose into Darcy's arm.

"Children Youth and Families are watching him," Margaret replied. "They're the ones who put him in 4-H. He's getting counseling. From all I hear he's doing pretty well right now."

I got up and went back to the door. "What do you think of Toby, Buster?"

"Judging by his smell and the way Painter reacts to him, Margaret's right."

"But with Bonehead loose..."

"Not much we can do about that," replied Buster. "Except be ready to chase him off if he turns up."

Darcy looked from me to Bob and Margaret. "Can I think about it?"

"Yes, but what we do with Belle will depend on your

decision," Margaret answered. "Please don't take too long making up your mind."

I came back to Darcy and put my front paws on her knee. She pulled me close.

"You have the softest little coat," she whispered.

No one spoke. I leaned against Darcy. Whatever choice she made was going to be terrifying for me.

She looked at Margaret. "Okay, I'll join 4-H and do agility through Pooch Patrol, even though it means working with Toby."

"You're sure," said Margaret.

"I'll ignore him."

Margaret frowned.

But Bob nodded his head at her. "Good decision, Darcy. I'm sure you can handle him."

I slid my front paws around Darcy's shoulders and dug my claws into her soccer fur. She gave me a hug. "Let's make the goal to get you trained enough to enter the 4-H agility class at the County Fair this summer, girl."

"That's a good goal," agreed Margaret. "You don't have to win a prize. Just complete the competition. Then she'll probably be disciplined and confident enough to behave in the yard."

Discipline again. Here came the scolding Buster and I were expecting. With a shudder, I slid to the floor and cowered. How could I get punished and be happy?

Margaret patted Darcy's shoulder. "I know it's hard not to be scared of Toby, but you know I wouldn't let you be around him if I thought he was still dangerous, don't you?"

What would she do if she knew Bonehead was loose?

Darcy nodded and swallowed.

"He knows he has to behave or his next stop will be a boy's home."

Darcy's mouth turned up at the corners. "Almost like Belle. She'll go to a new doggie home if she runs away again."

"That's right." Margaret scratched my ears. "Or dumps another waste basket around here."

Bob looked at Buster, a twinkle in his eye. "Or gets someone else worked up enough to knock off the grill grate."

They laughed, but I rolled onto my back. Time to be submissive. Punishment for both me and Buster had to be coming now that they were discussing our naughty behavior.

I glanced at Buster. His head hung low.

Darcy leaned down and reached toward me. "We won't let you go, Belle. We'll teach you some self-discipline."

Self-discipline? I had to punish myself? I squeezed my eyes tight shut.

She touched my belly and began to scratch. "How about a tummy rub?"

A what? Didn't discipline mean a reprimand, or time on my sleeping blanket?

She kept rubbing me. "Belle you're a good doggie. You're a good pet. Buster is, too. In fact, let's let him into the garage and we'll rub him dry. What do you say?"

We aren't getting punished? Buster might get to come in? I was getting another chance? Toby and Bonehead were in our lives again? Holy dog biscuits, life is confusing.

Chapter 5

Off on the Wrong Paw

I could hear Darcy singing as she entered the house. She did that more and more these days. Buster and I ran to greet her, tails wagging.

Breaking off in mid-melody, she bent and petted us. "Chorus is a ball, you guys. It's as much fun as karate, except it's different."

34

I looked at Buster. "What's a chorus?"

"A bunch of people singing, I guess. Must be loud."

Darcy resumed her song as she hung her coat and hurried down the hall. We scampered after her. When we reached her sleeping burrow, she hit a high note. That set my ears cringing. Buster whimpered, and I threw back my head and howled.

The note cracked and shattered into a laugh. "All right, you guys. I suppose I need to settle down and study before we go to Pooch Patrol tonight." She dropped onto her sleeping mat and bounced. "I've got to know whole notes and eighth notes and rests and quarter notes and let's see…"

She opened a notebook. "Oh yeah, time signatures and all the names of the notes. 'Cuz we're having a music test tomorrow." Bending, she rubbed my head. "Oh Belle, I hope you like agility. And I hope I ace my test." She flopped down and opened the notebook. "And I've got math and English tonight, too." She yawned. "It's hard when you take on something new isn't it?"

You got that right. It's scary, too. I jumped onto her bed and put my head on her knee. This whole agility thing reminded me of a bag of garbage. Some things you found tasted wonderful. Others made you puke. I had a hunch agility was both kinds.

Uncle Jim, Aunt Ellen, Painter, and – *holy fleas* – Toby picked Darcy, Buster, and me up after supper. We hadn't pulled away from Darcy's human den when I touched my nose to Painter's. "What's the latest on Bonehead?"

"They can't find him. Jim and I put some big poles up on the walking path."

"So Toby's staying with Aunt Ellen?"

"I guess. The people helping Ellen and Jim take care of him thought he'd be as safe with them as he would be any place." Painter scratched his ribs. "But Toby is never alone in the house now, and every time I bark, somebody's ready to call the cops."

What a horrible way to live. I hope Toby appreciates what Aunt Ellen and Uncle Jim are trying to do for him. If he doesn't I'll bite his ankle.

We got out of the car at the human den Toby called a 4-H Building.

"Hi," a round faced girl with short brown hair and bangs called out as Darcy led me inside.

Sniffing, I tried to detect Bonehead. But I could only smell horses that had once stood in stalls along one side of the den. I guess this place sat on the edge of town because I heard cows mooing beyond an open door.

If this agility thing doesn't work out, maybe I'll take off to join them. That way, I'll choose my new home, not Darcy and her parents. On the other paw, if Bonehead shows up, I should protect Darcy. I'd better make agility work.

"This is Darcy Simmons." Toby's voice broke into my thoughts.

He was talking to the round faced girl, who looked a few years older than Darcy. "I told you me and Ellen…uh, I and Ellen and Jim were bringing her tonight." He looked at Darcy. "This is J. J. Rogers. She and her dog won the 4-H state agility championship two years in a row."

Moving closer to Darcy, I wished Toby would go away.

J. J.'s brown eyes lighted, and she smiled at Darcy. "Welcome to Pooch Patrol. I'm a junior leader here." She pointed to a small stout woman in a wind breaker, blue jeans and a baseball cap. A gray ponytail poked out of the back of it. "That's Cori. She's our adult leader. She's asked me to get you and Belle started tonight, while she works with the more advanced students."

"Good luck, Darcy." Toby jogged off join Uncle Jim in the middle of the arena. With a bunch of boys, they pulled jumps and a tire out of a pick up.

Darcy put me on the tab she bought out of her allowance yesterday and looked at J. J. "Which is your dog?"

"The big black poodle by the bleachers." Pointing to the seats, she clapped her hands. "Cheri, come! Let's show Belle and Darcy how to do some stuff."

One sniff and my heart sank. Cheri was the dog who lived on the farm next to the place where I lived as a puppy with Bonehead and Toby. Cheri was always off to a groomer's, as far as I'd ever known, and she'd always given me a snotty bark when I got too close to her humans' den. Now on top of Toby, I had to work with her, and keep my nose out for Bonehead.

That took the moldy bone. Just the thought of him made me want to run like fire was singing my tail.

Cheri trotted to J. J., a red rhinestone collar glittering on her neck. I fought the urge to show her my teeth.

J. J. pointed to a high blue and white fence. "Jump, Cheri."

Cheri took off without a tab, following the direction of J. J.'s arm. Catching up to her, J. J. ran by her side. As Cheri finished the jump, J. J. looked at a thing that looked like a pointed hill. "A-frame."

Cheri pranced up one side and down the other pausing just before she jumped off.

I had to admit she looked like she knew how agility worked. But what did she think of me now? Lowering my ears, I studied her and hovered close to Darcy.

Cheri focused on J. J.

J. J. turned to Darcy. "Those yellow stripes at the bottom of the A-frame, the teeter-totter and the dog walk are contact areas. Your dog has to have at least one paw there getting on and getting off."

"Why?" Darcy stroked me.

"Safety. They have to slow down to place their paws right, so they're less apt to slip getting on and off the equipment.

I remembered our dash up the teeter-totter at Aunt Ellen's. If we'd gone slow, would I have avoided falling? Probably not. I tumbled when the teeter-totter dropped.

No way would I get on the one in the corner of this place.

But the A-frame looked like fun and I pulled Darcy toward it. The steep way up startled me. I stopped. Darcy tugged the tab.

"Let go," J. J. suggested. "Guide her by holding your hand along side her. Say 'A-frame' so she learns the command."

I felt better when Darcy let me find my own path to the top, while she reminded me where I was. I started down with a leap that catapulted me into the air. Landing hard, I nearly fell on Cheri.

The black poodle jumped aside. "Plant your feet at the bottom," she laughed.

Was she making fun of me? I let out a low growl.

She lifted her ears. "Hey! I know you."

"What of it?" Ready to fight if she got snotty, I shoved my nose against hers.

"You look like you got rescued, that's what." She wagged her pom-pom tail. "Welcome to agility. I hope you like it."

Well, of all the dog biscuits. I took a good sniff of her. She smelled like sweet cake. Maybe she could be civil when she felt like it. All right then, so could I. "Thank you, I hope so too."

Darcy turned me back to the A-frame. I ran up as she held her hand along side me. As I started down, she took my tab.

"Put your paw right in that yellow spot," Cheri called.

I did. This time my dismount was more a step than a leap.

"See? It's easy. Now watch this." She ran as J. J. motioned her to a jump.

Maybe she wasn't so bad. I'd been pretty rotten as a pup, living with Bonehead and Toby. Maybe I shouldn't blame her for driving me away from her humans' den.

Darcy pulled me toward the jump. "Over."

I managed to take off with her holding the tab, though I

didn't like her steering me. When I landed we headed for the tire.

Ha! She'd have to let go for now.

As I sailed through, I saw her facing the dog walk.

This was the cool thing that Aunt Ellen said made me look good. Evading Darcy's hand, I hurled myself toward the ramp ready to show my stuff.

"Belle, stop. Sit." Darcy shouted. "Stay!"

She was using her obey me now voice. I dropped to my haunches. *What was wrong?*

Painter hopped off the dog walk, veering so close to me that his fur brushed mine.

"Watch it, Belle," he said.

Toby's boot nicked my ribs. I screeched. Where had he come from?

Darcy glared at him, a peppery odor mixing with her flowery scent.

"Sorry," he exclaimed, hopping on one foot. "I didn't do it on purpose."

Yeah, right. Ribs smarting, I bared my teeth. That flea brain hadn't changed a bit.

Cheri rushed up. "Be careful Belle! You have to watch for other dogs during practice."

I turned to her and glared. Maybe she wasn't so civil after all.

"Wait for the dog coming down before you send yours up, Darcy," J. J. explained. "If Toby had collided with you, both of you could have been hurt."

Darcy put her hands on her hips. "I wanted to send her through the tunnel. She got away from me."

"Then turn her toward the tunnel, for crying out loud," Toby snapped, catching his breath. "Or hang on to her until you learn how to turn her."

He gave off a scared smell, like sweat on a sick person.

Darcy folded her arms. "Give me a chance. I'll bet you make your share of mistakes."

Uncle Jim walked up. "Toby, calm down." He gave

Darcy a sharp look. "We're going around the obstacles counter-clock wise."

That was Uncle Jim – saying what was on his mind. I wondered if he'd ever heard the word polite.

Darcy winced. I felt heat coming off her body, and her peppery smell got stronger.

J. J. patted her shoulder. "It's okay. Nothing horrible happened. Hang on to Belle until she gets used to the equipment. Let her have her head only if she's having trouble."

Darcy nodded. "Okay." Cheeks reddening, she looked at Uncle Jim. "Sorry, I'll be more careful."

He walked back to the bleachers.

Cheri gave me an approving nod. "You sat when she told you to, Belle. She's got good control of you."

Control? No! This was my time to run and play. Tucking my tail between my legs, I sulked.

J. J. looked at Cheri. "Tunnel."

She took off toward the round entrance. When she emerged on the other side, Darcy pulled my tab.

"Tunnel, Belle."

She had to let me go at the entrance and I shot in. Maybe if I moved fast enough, she couldn't catch me on the other side.

Not a chance in dog heaven. Her fingers closed on the tab before I was fully on my feet at the exit. We headed for the A-frame again. I planted my paws on the bottom then tugged, hoping she'd let me go.

"No Belle," she whispered.

Looks like if I wanted to stay with her, I'd better accept the tab. *Rabid skunks!*

Darcy eased me over the A-frame's point. I pouted as I walked down the other side making me miss putting my paws on the yellow stripe.

"Wrong, Belle," Darcy said. "Do it again."

I growled under my breath.

Near us, Toby steered Painter toward a low block of

40

wood. "Table."

When Painter hopped onto it, Toby stepped back. "Stay."

Looking up at Darcy he called, "Pull up on her where you want her to put her paws. When she steps in the right place, say 'contact.'"

Her eyes straight ahead, she held me so I had no choice but to stop where she wanted me to as I went up and down the A-frame.

"There. That's better." she muttered, starting toward a fence. "Now jump."

I got ready to leap, but she veered wide around the obstacle, dragging me with her. I ran around the fence.

Toby chuckled. "Stretch your arm toward her as you go and she'll hop over."

"You don't have to laugh at me," Darcy pulled me back around to the front of the jump.

"He's not," said J. J. "He's right,"

Toby grinned. "I did the same thing when I first tried with Painter. Almost pulled him off his feet."

I looked at Painter still on the platform and spoke so only he could hear. "How did that feel?"

"Pretty bad at the time, but it's funny now."

"Come," Toby called him.

Uncle Jim walked to Darcy and pointed to the bleachers where Aunt Ellen sat. "I think you and Belle need a break." A peppery smell rolled off him, and he stuck out his lower lip.

I strained toward the seats. When he looked like that, we'd better obey.

Face turning red and her own pepper rising, Darcy led me to where Aunt Ellen sat with Buster at her feet.

He wagged his tail. "My turn?"

"Yes," I growled. "The course is all yours."

Shooting Uncle Jim a stern look, Aunt Ellen put her arm around Darcy and patted me. "I'll talk to him."

Darcy gulped back a sob. "I don't want to be around

41

Toby."

"I understand." Aunt Ellen looked at her and sighed. "Uncle Jim has no idea what it would be like to be a girl and go through what you did, especially from Toby's father."

Darcy burst into tears. Perhaps Aunt Ellen's kindness made her cry, or perhaps her anger at Toby and his father did it.

"M-m-maybe this a-agility thing is a s-s-stupid idea, Aunt Ellen," sobbed Darcy.

Aunt Ellen pulled a tissue from her pocket and gave it to Darcy. "How 'bout you, Toby, and I sit down together and the two of you talk a little bit one of these days?"

Wiping her eyes, Darcy stared at me. "B-Belle doesn't s-seem to want to l-learn agility. She's unhappy, Aunt Ellen. Maybe she does need to be out on a farm someplace."

No, please! Heart dropping to my stomach, I pushed my head under Darcy's hand.

"Maybe she needs to do agility a few times, to see if she likes it."

"I don't know," Darcy moaned.

Aunt Ellen raised a brow. "Perhaps a little patience will help you succeed."

Darcy shrugged.

"Think about it." Her aunt gave her a squeeze.

Darcy sat down on the ground, put her arms around me, and dried her tears on my shoulder. "It isn't fair that I should have to deal with Toby to keep Belle."

Aunt Ellen didn't respond.

Heaving a long sigh and biting her lip, Darcy turned her glance from me.

I let out my own deep breath and looked toward the ring.

Big dogs and little ones raced around it, a blur of browns, blacks, whites, beiges, and grays. As they leaped, dove, and wriggled among obstacles, their owners shouted encouragement.

Painter marched across the dog walk, while Toby waited at the other end. Cheri ran at J. J.'s command and burrowed in the tunnel. The whirling mass and the roar it made gave me a head ache. I took a deep breath and let it out.

The cow aroma drifted through the open door, warm and strong, mingling with the crisp smell of approaching frost. Hoping for nights with Darcy in front of a fire, I inhaled again.

Phew! A barfy, rotten-fruit stench filled my nose. Bonehead! Very near. My hackles rose, and pulling away from Darcy I pointed my nostrils toward the dark stalls. Did he rustle in those shadows? A growl rumbled in my throat.

"Belle," Darcy whispered. "Take it easy."

I let my ears swivel left, right.

"Weave poles," called Toby to Painter.

Cheri rode the teeter-totter to the ground. As she stepped off, she spoke so only I could hear. "It gets better Belle. I felt like you did once."

That didn't matter right now. I kept my eyes on the shadows. They didn't move. Bonehead's stench began to lessen. Was he outside?

Darcy looked at my twitching nostrils. "What do you smell, girl?"

If you only knew. My brain felt as confused as my nose. Where was he? Holy bones, Darcy. I can't leave you. We can't give up on each other.

I pointed my ears toward the door, straining to screen out the dogs and people running in the arena. Outside, footsteps faded. So did the odor.

Thank you dog heaven. He's not in the stalls. I pushed my nose hard against Darcy's leg and rubbed my cheek on her knee.

She lifted me into her arms. "I love you, Belle." Her lips brushed against my ear. "I'll sleep on things tonight, girl. Decide what we should do."

Whimpering, I licked her chin.

Chapter 6

Between a Porcupine and a Prickle Bush

Curling onto his bed in Darcy's sleeping burrow, Buster laid his chin on his paws. "I'm beat after all that agility stuff. Are you, Belle?"

I could only groan. Every joint ached, and my eyes burned. But though I'd turned three times on my own blanket and dropped onto my belly, I couldn't close my eyes.

Down the hall in the food burrow, Darcy, Bob, and Margaret's voices rose and fell. I caught the words 'Uncle Jim' and 'Toby.' Beyond that, the walls muffled everything else anyone said. Only their scents drifted to me. Darcy smelled of fear and sadness, like wilted flowers and sick sweat. Margaret and Bob smelled caring and warm, like the aroma a clean nest might be.

They had been talking ever since we came home from Pooch Patrol. Were they deciding if she would continue to take me there? Or what to do with me if we didn't go any more? I shivered from my head to my tail.

Buster began to snore, and I gave him an envious look. He thrived wherever he sprawled. If I could do that, would I be in less trouble? Probably. On the other paw, he had a future. Why shouldn't he be happy?

Sighing, I curled up and tried to snuggle into my blanket, but it bunched hard under my haunches. I pawed it, but it didn't soften. Maybe I should stretch out on the floor.

As I slid onto the rug, I realized the talk had stopped. Darcy's step's tapped and she appeared in the sleeping burrow door, the wilted flower scent clinging to her. Glancing at the school bag on her desk, she grimaced.

Buster opened his eyes.

Darcy looked at me. "Belle, let me fix your bed." Kneeling, she shook out and refolded my blanket. "There." She stifled a yawn.

I touched my whiskers to her wrist in thanks and stood beside her, waiting for her next move.

Settling on the floor between Buster and me, she stroked my head. "Mom and Dad just told me Toby's father broke out of jail." She put one arm around me. "I'd like to quit doing Pooch Patrol, but there's just no way I can get to the other agility place." She drew a breath. "We talked and talked about it."

I braced to hear that Margaret and Bob would find me a new home.

Darcy slipped her hand into the pocket of her outer fur,

removed the cell phone she always carried, and studied it. "Dad says I should go on with Pooch Patrol. Call the cops if I see Mr. Johnson."

Buster and I slid our forelegs into her lap and leaned our heads against her shoulders. I licked her neck.

"We'll protect you," Buster said with a low woof.

Putting the phone away, she rubbed our ears. "Mom thinks I should try to get to know Toby."

I glanced at Buster and spoke in a voice only he could hear. "How could Margaret ask her to do that?"

He tapped his tail on the rug. "Toby's part of our family, since he lives with Uncle Jim and Aunt Ellen."

Holy bones! I nuzzled Darcy's knee, wishing I could change that.

She pulled me close. "I'm going to sit down with Toby tomorrow, Belle." Tears welled in her eyes. "I hate the idea, but otherwise I might as well give you away."

Oh, dog heaven. I snuggled in her arms.

Buster licked her ear. "It'll be all right. You'll see. Toby's cool." He put his head on her shoulder.

Darcy sniffed, wiped her cheek, and gazed at me.

I gave a tiny tail wag. Don't give me away, please.

She drew a deep breath and began to sing a slow sad song.

> "Got no idea if this'll work, Li'le Dog.
> Got no idea if this'll work, Li'le Dog --"

She paused.

What was she thinking? Was she changing her mind about talking to Toby?

The song began again.

> "Got no idee if this gonna work, Li'le
> friend. Got no idee if this gonna work,
> Li'le friend."

She pressed her cheek into my shoulder and whispered in my ear.

"But I'll be with you right to the bitter
end. Yeah, gonna be with you to the
bitter end."

She put her arms around us. "That's the Blues, guys. It's fun to sing 'cuz you can make up your own words when you're sad." The last word faded into another yawn. Putting her hand over her mouth, she rose and walked to her book bag. "I better quit horsin' around and get at my homework, guys, though I'd love to curl up with you for the night."

Buster and Painter lay beside me on Aunt Ellen's food burrow floor, while she washed dishes. Darcy and Toby sat face-to-face at the human eating table, a plate of homemade cookies between them. Misty batted a string of feathers attached to a rod.

Stupid cat. Playing away while people discussed my fate.

Toby bit into a raspberry pinwheel and pushed the plate toward Darcy.

Shaking her head, she curled her fingers in her lap.

I scrunched across the floor and licked her foot.

She leaned down, scratched my ears, then took a deep breath and looked up at Toby. "So why did you come bothering me and Belle in the park last summer?"

He dunked his cookie into a glass of milk. "'Cuz my dad was there. He made me do a lot of the stuff I did."

Yeah, right. I pressed closer to Darcy. When Toby spotted her in Maryville Park, he pointed her out to Bonehead. I felt like snapping at his ankle. Instead, I put my front paws on Darcy's lap.

Aunt Ellen turned off the water and faced Toby.

He glanced at her then back at Darcy. "Okay, I started messing with you before my dad did. I was stupid."

Darcy put her arms around me. Climbing onto her thighs, I put my head on her shoulder. "Couldn't you have – like – stopped him," she asked.

"He'd have walloped me," Toby looked at his hands. "He used to do it all the time. He'll do it again as soon as he can, now that he's escaped from jail."

I almost felt sorry for him. Who'd want Bonehead kicking them around?

Stroking me, Darcy looked at Toby. "Where's your mom? Can't she help you?"

"She's in the state women's prison." Toby scoffed. "She's as mean as Dad."

Darcy stared at the cookies.

They smelled delicious, and I stretched to taste them, but she held me back. "So now what will you do?"

Toby shrugged. "Go to school and Pooch Patrol, I guess."

She looked doubtful. "What happened when the cops picked you up last summer?"

"They sent me to Rock River Boot Camp." He grimaced. "Not fun."

"It's not supposed to be," she retorted. "What did they do with you?"

"If you were sassy, they made you march. The first week, I did eleven hours of marching."

"All at once?"

"No, it was like detention after school every day." Toby took a swallow of milk. "Then this counselor – Sergeant Reeves… He was cool, like my grandpa before he died. Grandpa had a way of saying what grownups wanted so it all made sense."

Biting into his cookie, Toby chewed and swallowed. "Sergeant Reeves was like that. He said I didn't have to be like my dad. So, I started working on stuff."

"Oh," Darcy said studying him.

He looked down. "I'm sorry about what I did to you and Belle. Honest."

He smelled sad, like old treat boxes after the last biscuit got eaten.

She pondered. "I guess you had it tough. I never thought about it."

"There was a lot of bad stuff at home," Toby sighed.

I rubbed my nose against her wrist. Toby did to us what other people did to him. I'd been pretty mean right after I lived with him and Bonehead. Darcy taught me better. Did Sergeant Reeves teach Toby better? I glanced at Buster.

His tail wag answered my un-woofed question.

Patting me, then him, Darcy sighed. "I guess I understand. You and Belle are a lot alike."

"Yeah, I guess we are," Toby wiped his fingers on a paper napkin.

I was like him? *Now wait a flea bitten minute.*

Neither spoke. Darcy selected a cookie and nibbled it. Both of them finished their milk.

Finally Toby glanced out the kitchen window. "Well, you want to set up the agility stuff?"

I held my breath.

She shrugged. "Yeah, let's."

Sweet dog heaven, I would stay with her a while longer. But, before I went out there to do tricks, I better get at least one cookie. Leaping onto the table, I pawed the plate. Cookies spun into the air.

Buster snatched two walnut and a vanilla before they hit the ground. Painter grabbed a ginger snap. I jumped down and scarfed snicker doodles from the floor.

Toby and Aunt Ellen burst out laughing.

Darcy opened the door. "Come on Belle, let's get you busy before you do any more damage."

Buster, Painter and Misty raced outside. I dragged behind them. When Darcy turned her back on me to help Toby set up the agility equipment, I bolted for the creek bank, to run while I had the chance, and to sniff out Bonehead if he lurked in the trees.

When they got the course set, I hid under a bush. Darcy

hooked Buster to her tab. He lolloped through the tire, over the dog walk, and up and down the A-frame. When he got to the weave poles, he sent them sprawling in every direction.

Misty mewed with delight.

"Hunker down and skim around them," I shouted at him.

Tongue lolling he yelled back, "Stop goofing off and come here."

I hadn't smelled Bonehead anywhere around, so I had no excuse to linger. Sighing, I slunk up the lawn to Darcy.

She attached the tab to my collar and ran toward a jump. "Belle, over."

I cleared the hurdle.

"Good! Tunnel."

Her praise gave me energy. I bounded to the tunnel entrance. She let the tab go, and I dived in. The slick floor set me skidding. Feet shooting from under me, I slid through on my butt.

Darcy and Toby roared as I popped out, dug my claws into the grass, and stopped.

"Get down on your belly," Painter woofed. "Then you won't slip."

I mustered my best look of wounded dignity. "Now you tell me."

Darcy guided me to the weave poles, encouraging me into a tight corner around the first one.

For a moment I felt better. Herding dogs cut corners from the time they walk, so I got that part fast. But then I couldn't figure out what to do when I came around a pole. I kept wanting to go straight, but each time, Darcy turned me around.

"Weave, Belle weave," she said until I felt dizzy.

Misty pranced up and wove in and out, rubbing her back on each pole. "It's easy. What's your problem?"

Catty show off.

Toby and Painter trotted up. "It's okay, Belle." Painter

touched his nose to mine. "The weave poles are tough to learn."

"Weave Painter," commanded Toby. "Try it without a tab."

Painter rounded the first pole away from Toby, and the next coming toward him. Then he twined around the third pole, but instead of turning into the fourth, he went straight and ran along side the poles.

"No. Uh – wrong." Toby said. "Come on, let's do it again."

Painter looked as befuddled as I had, but before I could sympathize with him, Darcy steered me toward a table like the one at Pooch Patrol I hopped onto it.

She dropped the tab. "Stay," she said and took three steps back.

Jumping down, I followed her.

"Wrong," She returned me to the table. "Belle, stay."

Dog biscuits. My ear itched, but I couldn't scratch because of another stupid rule! But I'd better obey; otherwise she'd make me sit here all the longer, or worse, send me to that farm.

"Good dog, come." She waved a treat that smelled like bacon.

I bounced to her, itch forgotten, and lifted the treat from her fingers. On the other paw, obeying was sometimes worth the trouble to do it.

When I finished eating, we raced to more fences. Stretching long, I sailed over the broad jump and a log. My muscles felt terrific as I landed. I had to admit, I liked this one part of agility.

I turned to race the other way over the jumps, but Darcy clapped her hands. "That's enough, Belle," she called, and turned to Toby. "I'm going to take a break and try to do some homework."

Aww, dog biscuits. I pranced beside her. Don't stop now.

She walked to the porch, dropped onto the steps, and

dug in the bag where she kept her school books.

Nodding to her, Toby jogged down the lawn. "Come on, Painter, let's practice weaving."

I nuzzled Darcy. "Take me on the jumps again, please. Just once more."

Smiling a little she pushed my nose aside, and opened a book. "Sit, Belle. I need to start my science questions. We can do more agility later."

I plopped my front paws on her lap, shoving the book to the ground. "Come on Darcy," I whimpered. "Let's jump."

"Down," she ordered, shoving me harder. "And don't ruin my book, or Mom won't let me take it over here." She picked it up and brushed dirt off the cover. "Then I'll really have a time getting everything completed for school."

I lowered my ears and watched her. *What had I done wrong by asking to do more jumping?* Sighing as she began to read, I lay down and stared at the yard.

Buster snuffled near the creek, and romped in and out of the water. Painter practiced on the dog walk. The empty jumps gleamed in the sunlight.

Rotten meat, why couldn't I be out there? Wait! I could. I could jump by myself? Leaping to my feet, I charged down the grass to the highest fence and flung myself over it.

Misty sauntered out of the bushes. "Knock a bar down and you're a rotten bone," she challenged.

"You're on, kitty cat." I spun and soared over the rail from the other direction. Back and forth I raced until I gasped for air and would have knocked a bar down if I hadn't stopped to catch my breath.

Misty paraded to the teeter-totter and climbed to the top, tail in the air. "Come up here and get me."

Was she kidding? I dropped to my haunches.

Buster exploded out of the shrubs by the creek. "I'll get you, Misty."

Painter paused in the middle of the dog walk turned

and looked at him.

"Come," Toby called.

Painter didn't respond.

"Painter!" Toby clapped his hands.

Snapping his head around, Painter ran to the ground, but kept one eye on Buster.

Toby patted Painter. "Good dog. Take a break. Go get Misty."

Leaves flew as Painter took off. Together he and Buster roared up the teeter totter. Misty jumped off and ran. They rode down, barking for the fun of it.

How could they do that? Stomach feeling like I'd eaten a snow ball, I raced back to the porch and cowered against Darcy.

Putting her book aside, she stroked me. "Okay, Belle. I'll finish science later. It's too distracting to work here." She watched Painter and Buster jump off the teeter. "That's the one piece of equipment we haven't tried yet, Belle. Let's go do it."

Oh, dog heaven. Tail between my legs, I tried to pull away from her, but she marched me forward. "Belle, teeter-totter."

I put my paw in the yellow contact zone at the bottom, then crept up the teeter's slope. The board wobbled. Bracing my paws, I began to shake. This thing seemed to touch the sky. When it fell, would I fly off like before?

"Come on, Belle, teeter-totter," Darcy coaxed. Letting go of the tab, she held up a hand to guide me as I walked.

I thought about jumping, but the ground looked far away. Swallowing terror, I extended one fore leg, then one back leg.

The teeter-totter creaked. Closing my eyes and bracing my legs, I waited for the board to drop.

Thud! The teeter hit the ground, rattling my joints. Heart pounding, I leaped off without looking where I went, and catapulted into Buster.

He yelped, and we both rolled on the grass.

Darcy pulled me off him. "Belle, take it easy."

Take it easy? Never. Even for a million bacon flavored biscuits. You bring me near that teeter-totter again, and I'll run until I find the land of the wild dogs. Catching my breath, I gave her the unhappiest look I could manage.

She laughed. "Weave poles and teeter-totters, Belle. That's what we have to work on the hardest. Everything else went much better today than it did at Pooch Patrol."

She had that right, but I fought the urge to slip my head out of my collar and run away. Of course, if I did that, Darcy wouldn't keep me, and I had to be nearby in case Bonehead showed up.

Rabid cats! Why couldn't I just do the easy fun parts of agility to earn my place with her, and leave the rest alone?

Chapter 7

Frustration

"Well, Margaret, did you ever think we'd have toilet plungers back here?" Bob looked at eight round bottomed tall sticks he'd put in the yard.

She laughed. "No, but they'll be perfect weave poles."

"Thanks, Dad," Darcy put the tab on my collar. "Come on, Belle. Weave."

I trotted onto the frost hardened ground. Thank dog heaven Bob hadn't figured out how to make a teeter totter.

"What about your homework, Darcy?" Margaret tightened the thick outer fur she wore now that the cold time had come. "You've got Pooch Patrol tonight, remember."

"I've got most of it done I'll finish up the rest when I get home."

Margaret frowned. "You've been up awfully late these past few nights, between working with Belle and karate practice."

"I'm okay in the morning." She guided me toward a pole. "Weave, Belle."

I circled, felt a tug on the tab and came back toward Darcy. She slacked the small leash, and I swung around the next pole.

Margaret glanced at her watch. "I would like your lights out by 9:30 from now on, please."

"It's okay. I'm able to concentrate in school." Darcy's tone took on an edge. "Come on, Mom."

Margaret folded her arms.

"I beg your pardon," Bob said.

Wilting, Darcy stifled a sigh. "Okay, I'll be there in a minute. I'm sorry."

Margaret went into the food burrow. Bob followed.

Darcy bent close to me. "Belle, weave one more time, quick."

I trotted around the first pole, alert for her next command. The sooner we finished, the sooner she'd get out of trouble, and I'd get off this frozen ground into the human den.

Something clattered. I swung my head toward the sound. Buster lolloped behind us, scattering the plungers as he bounced.

He looked so funny I forgot what I was doing and missed a turn.

"Wrong, Belle." Darcy pulled me. "Pay attention. Never mind Buster."

I focused, and we finished the line.

Darcy reset the poles and ran Buster around them. They flew in every direction a second time.

She laughed. "Buster at the rate you're going, you'll never be an agility dog."

He cocked his head at her and let his tongue flop.

She scratched his ears. "Yeah, your future doesn't depend on agility."

Lucky him. What will mine finally be? I trotted across the porch and scratched at the back door.

Bob let me in. The food burrow smelled like chicken. Licking my chops I looked for a piece of something to grab.

Ah! There was skin in the garbage can. Nose wiggling, I stepped toward it.

Buster barked. Margaret let him in.

Remembering my promise to him, I walked to my dishes and drank water.

"Good dog, Belle." Margaret smiled. "Good choice."

Darcy came in, took off her heavy outer fur, grabbed an apple and headed for her sleeping den. Buster and I followed and lay on the floor beside her. I rested my chin on her foot.

Yawning, she patted us. "Mom's right. I need more sleep. I may have to give up singing and go back to study hall. Managing all my work without one is harder than I thought it would be."

Holy bones! I lifted my head and stared at her. She would give up singing? For me? Okay, at Pooch Patrol tonight, I'll listen to her every command. I'll master those weave poles.

But J. J. waved Darcy, Toby, Cheri, Buster, and me over to the teeter-totter when we arrived at the 4-H building. My heart sank as Darcy guided me onto the board while the others watched. Up I climbed, the tab tugging at my collar.

Darcy, let go. If I slip, I want to be able to jump off. I cringed.

She pulled me forward. "Come on, Belle. It's okay."

The teeter dropped, and my stomach with it. Yanking free of her I sprang off and rolled onto my back. *Please don't make me do this.*

"She's really scared of that thing," mused J. J. "We have to get her over it, or she can't enter competitions."

I had to do the teeter in an agility class? Oh fleas. I hung my head.

Darcy stroked me. "Please don't quit, Belle. I love you."

Toby looked at her. "Maybe if you walk her up, and J. J. and I slowly guide the teeter-totter down, she can get used to it."

With a frown, Darcy looked at J. J.

"That's a good suggestion, Toby," J. J. answered.

I lowered my ears and tail. Don't make me work with Toby, please.

Toby smiled.

"Okay," Darcy said. Pointing me toward the teeter-totter, she whispered, "I've got to give him a chance, girl."

Dog heaven don't let him hurt me. I slunk to the top. J. J. and Toby eased the teeter to the ground. My stomach stayed in place, and I didn't fall, but what would happen when I landed at normal speed?

Darcy guided me off and gave me a treat. "Good dog."

They reset the teeter and Darcy led me up it again. This time they let the teeter-totter fall harder. My stomach lurched, but I stayed on, and stepped off straight when it landed, paws touching the yellow stripe.

"Perfect," woofed Painter and Buster together.

"I'm proud of you," said Cheri.

I'd sure had the wrong idea about her. Now that I was civil, she was as kind as she could be. Toby wasn't being mean either. Maybe he was getting nicer. Maybe it was for real.

"This time, do it without any help," J. J. said.

I walked part way up, then caught a glimpse of the ground. If I tumbled from here, I'd break my legs. A shiver running from my nose to my tail, I stepped carefully.

"You're fine." Cheri barked. "Right in the middle. Stay there."

The board tipped, and my heart began to thump. The teeter hit the ground with the jolt I hated. Leaping off, I missed the yellow stripe and stumbled.

"Walk off," Cheri said. "Otherwise, you could hurt yourself."

J. J. folded her arms. "Make her do it again, Darcy."

Oh, dog heaven, no.

But Darcy tugged the tab, and up the middle of the teeter I went.

"That's right," called Painter.

But when the teeter dropped, I still half sprung off. One paw brushed the yellow stripe when I scrambled to solid ground.

"Good dog." Darcy bent and hugged me. "That was better." She smiled at Toby. "Thanks."

I felt like biting both of them.

J. J. scratched my ears. "Practice will make you less afraid, girl."

No it won't. I'll never get used to that thing. I mustered my saddest look.

"Go do something else now," suggested J. J, giving me another pat. "Come back here later."

Yes! I strained toward a row of fences. Let's do jumps.

Darcy tugged me away from them. "You can jump with your eyes closed, Belle. Let's do the stuff you need to work on."

Oh bones.

"Tunnel," she said

Okay. I'd settle for that. It meant a little time off the tab.

Dropping onto my belly I slid through the tunnel. When I got out, I wheeled and scuttled back through the other way, stretching the moment.

Darcy dashed to catch my tab, and guided me to the table. "Stay."

I did, head high.

"Come, Belle."

I bounced to her, then spun to race back to make her call me again.

She caught my tab before I could escape. "Let's do the A-frame and dog walk."

J. J. watched us. "You're doin' good, Belle." To Darcy she said, "You should bring her to the Dog Jamboree after the holidays."

"What's that?" Darcy tossed me a treat.

"You run an agility course and get a score from a judge like at a show, except the Jamboree's just for practice."

Darcy looked down at me. "You want to try that, Belle?"

Not really. But I would, of course. It was all part of staying with her.

"Why don't you kick the challenge up a notch," J. J. suggested. "Run her off a tab when you practice. See how she does."

Off a tab? Holy dog heaven! That would be fun. Cocking my ears and wagging my tail, I looked as bright eyed and cute as possible.

"She does like being off tab." Darcy patted my head.

"Then start training her without one."

Training? I knew how to behave off lead. What was J. J. thinking?

Darcy kept rubbing me. "Good idea. We'll start tomorrow."

I pushed my nose into her hand. Why not tonight? We'd run like we did in the park when she wore her wheeled shoes. I'd jump the fences.

"Sit, Belle," she said. "It's Buster's turn to work now."

Buster? I glanced at him flopped down near us, head on his paws, eyes half closed. He didn't care a hoot about agility. Why should she turn to him?

Darcy unhooked my tab and attached it to his collar. "Come on boy."

Opening his eyes, he heaved a long sigh. "Aw dog biscuits."

I gave him my blackest look, then lay down and sulked.

He dismissed me with a flick of his tail and shambled after Darcy into the ring.

Chapter 8

Almost, But No Dog Biscuit

Following Toby, Darcy, Buster, and Painter I romped across Aunt Ellen's porch and into the yard.

"Okay, Belle," Darcy laughed. "Let's try you off tab."

"Off tab?" Misty, poked her head around Aunt Ellen's legs. "Let me out. I want to see this. I need a good laugh."

Aunt Ellen grabbed her. "You stay here. Let Belle practice in peace."

Excitement made me tingle from head to toe.

"Why don't we start with the jump right here." Toby pointed to a fence a few dog lengths away. "Then let's

61

go left to the dog walk, and right to the tire. Then there's another jump. Let's make that a trap."

"A what?" asked Darcy.

"A trap. Don't go over the jump even though it would be logical right after the tire," he said. "It's a trick to see if you and the dog can avoid an obstacle. Turn right and head for the A-frame. End with the teeter-totter."

I tucked my tail between my legs. Always the flea-bitten teeter-totter.

She frowned. "Is it a test to see if Belle will follow a command not to take a jump?"

"Sort of," said Toby. "It's designed to see if she's listening carefully, and only takes an obstacle on command."

Buster took the first run, with his usual carefree lollop. By the time he finished, two jumps lay on the ground, and three weave poles sprawled, but he didn't miss a single contact point.

Darcy panted as she brought him back to the porch. "You are one tough dog to handle, even with a tab. Maybe I should forget showing you."

Buster yawned and flopped down on the porch, tail thumping. Whatever she wanted would be fine with him, I was sure.

Painter ran the course easily, missing one contact point on the A-frame.

"Wrong." Toby made him go again.

I had to admit Toby seemed to be getting nicer when Painter messed up.

Darcy led me to the starting spot, and I bolted for the first jump. "Hey! Wrong," she called. "I have to send you off. Come back here."

I returned, ears lowered. Another stupid rule.

She made me sit for what seemed like forever, then pointed toward the jump. "Over."

As I sailed across the obstacle, I smelled her moving toward the dog walk.

"Contact," she called.

Touching the walk's yellow stripe, I pranced across.

"Good dog," Darcy shouted. "Tire."

I dove through the tire, the wind in my ears. It brought a delicious aroma from Aunt Ellen's food burrow. Darcy's parents would come for supper after practice. Painter, Misty, Buster and I would play. How much fun that would be? Joyfully, I landed.

Darcy called "A frame." But I flew at the forbidden jump.

"Wrong, Belle. A-frame," Darcy shouted.

I knew I should turn around, but running was so much fun! Over the jump I soared, wind tickling my ears. Watch out, you birds.

My fore paws slammed onto the ground. The force of the landing shot them from under me. Before I could think, I rolled toward the creek. The ground dropped away, and I crashed into cold water. Barks and shrieks of human laughter echoed as I scrambled to my feet and shook.

Darcy ran toward me and grabbed my collar "Wrong, Belle. Bad dog."

I caught a mild but peppery smell on her. *Oh bones, I'd goofed. Big time.* She'd start looking for a farmer who wants a dog, if I did that again.

"Put her tab back on," called Toby.

No. Don't do that, please.

"Teeter-totter," Darcy said, ignoring him.

Dripping mud, I made sure I stepped on the yellow stripe, then climbed, slowing near the crash spot. The teeter-totter tilted, and I hung on for the slam. When it came, I carefully stepped into the contact zone.

"Okay, that's better," said Darcy.

Thank you, thank you. I licked her hand.

She rubbed my head, then turned to Toby. "Can a trap change from run to run?"

"Yup." He nodded. "It's good to change them so the dogs will learn to not run at any obstacle unless you tell it to."

She grinned. "Then how 'bout the A-frame is the trap now? We'll send the dogs over the jump, to the weave poles and to the teeter-totter."

"Okay," he nodded. "Why don't you let me take Buster around for fun? See if I can make him finish with the course in one piece."

She shrugged. "Why not?"

He and Painter ran the course with no trouble. Then Toby took hold of Buster's tab. "Let's go, boy."

I had two good eyes, but I still hardly believed what I saw next. Buster's lollop turned to a gallop as he and Toby sped toward the first jump.

Tail streaming behind him, Buster soared over, completed the dog walk, and headed for the tire. Before I knew it he had finished it and the next jump, ignored the A-frame trap, and headed for the weave poles. He scattered four of them, but managed the teeter totter.

"What got into you," I exclaimed when he came back to the porch.

His tongue lolled at me. "That was great. I love running with Toby."

"What's wrong with going with Darcy?"

"She's not fast enough."

"Buster, you're a clown."

"You should talk," he retorted.

"No girl can run as fast as a boy," I said. "You're mean."

Painter growled. "You're opinionated."

"I am not. Herding dogs defend the people and animals they're responsible for."

Darcy clapped her hands. "All right, come here, Belle. Get ready."

I focused on her words and smells, ready to do my best to keep off the tab.

She sat me on the starting spot. "Belle, Go. Jump."

I smelled her beside me again as I ran, and swiveled my ears in that direction.

"Dog walk," she said.

Tearing across the yard, I completed the obstacle. She called for the tire, and I shot through it.

"Good dog," she said, pointing to the fence right beyond the tire. "Jump."

Jump? There? I got in trouble once for doing that.

She kept pointing. "Jump."

All right. I ran and sprang, nostrils flaring, expecting her peppery anger, but she smelled like happy flowers. "Good dog, Belle. Good dog. Now weave."

I got around the first pole, then ran straight down the row.

"Wrong," Darcy called.

I straggled around the poles again, missing about half of them.

Together Darcy and I raced for the A-frame. I scrambled over it, touching the contact zone both times.

"Hey!" Toby yelled. "That's a trap, remember?"

"Darn," Darcy exclaimed, turning around. "Belle, come."

I gave her a sour look. You called for it. Don't blame me.

She patted my head. "I'm sorry. That was my fault."

She looked so sad that I pushed my nose into her hand.

"Teeter-totter," Darcy commanded.

I marched up the teeter's slope. When it hit the ground, I stepped off properly, though I still hated the bone rattling landing.

Darcy rubbed my back. "Good Belle. You paid attention to me. We both goofed but we'll get better. I'm going to leave you off the tab."

Holy dog biscuits. Thank you. Jumping up, I licked her face. Together we walked up to the porch and Toby.

He glanced at the sky. "The sun's going down and your folks will be here soon. It's probably time to stop."

Darcy gave me a final pat. "Okay, I'll help put the equipment away."

Together they walked down the lawn.

I watched them go. Life was certainly easier since they

were getting along.

Painter and Buster walked up and lay down next to where I stood. "You're doin' good, Belle, keep it up," said Painter.

"I don't get traps, Painter." I licked dirt from between my toes.

He wagged his tail. "Never assume you're supposed to take every obstacle. Go only on command. Then you'll avoid any traps."

"What if Darcy sends me to a trap instead of around it?"

"Then it's her mistake, not yours."

So much to learn. Would I ever get it all down? Still, I reflected. "Traps aside, I think today's the best I've ever done."

"Good," said Buster, stretching beside Painter. "Then I guess everything's okay."

Yes, it was. Heaving a contented sigh, I flopped on my side between my friends. I guess I had reason to be pretty proud of myself today. Maybe staying with Darcy was a real possibility. Stretching out, I closed my eyes.

For a long time I lay quiet, listening to the wind rustling the bushes by the house, and smelling something delicious in the food burrow.

Then a peppery, sick sweat stench washed over me, and something splashed in the creek.

Buster lifted his ears. "What was that? Did Darcy or Toby fall in?"

"No!" I exclaimed, shooting to my feet, "Smell! That's Bonehead."

Buster sniffed. "Holy bones, you're right. He's trying to cross the creek. Come on."

With a snarl, we tore down the lawn.

"Darcy," Toby yelled from somewhere near the weave poles. "My dad's here. Run."

She dropped the bar of a jump and raced up the lawn. Toby followed.

I waited until they reached the food burrow door, then

plunged after my friends.

Thundering, they stood in the middle of the steam. Bonehead scrambled onto the opposite shore.

I let out a roaring bark as I joined Buster and Painter. Bursting onto the bank, we chased Bonehead into the trees.

A dog length ahead of us, he shinned up a trunk, crawled onto a limb and dropped over a tall fence.

"Knock it down," I bellowed.

We charged the barrier, slamming into it with a crash. It shuddered and held fast.

"No way," gasped Painter, and sank into a pile of leaves, sides heaving. "Absolutely no way."

Buster dropped beside him. "Rotten meat!"

I let out a final snarl. "Don't worry. One of these times, we'll catch him and when we do, we'll make him wish he'd never sprung out of jail. Good try, guys. Good try."

Chapter 9

Discovery

Two cops stood in Aunt Ellen's food burrow. One looked as tall as a tree. The other was short with thick arms.

"No sign of him, I'm sorry," the tall one said.

"Rats," groaned Toby.

Aunt Ellen, Margaret, Bob, and Darcy sighed.

Uncle Jim put a hand on Toby's shoulder. "If he comes back we'll call you again."

"I'm afraid that's all you can do." replied the short cop. "Good night." Nodding to Uncle Jim, he walked out the door. His partner followed.

No one spoke. Darcy, Margaret, and Aunt Ellen began setting human dishes on the table, while Uncle Jim and Bob meandered into the living room.

Silverware clattered. The TV came on. From it's roar, the men had found some game they called football. Then Aunt Ellen looked at Darcy and Toby and spoke, "How about the homework, you kids? If it's not done, there's time before supper."

"I need to read some stuff." Darcy yawned.

Margaret took a stack of people dishes from her. "Then go read," she said gently.

Toby fed us and opened the door to let us out. "I got the same assignment she does."

"Then you go too," smiled Aunt Ellen. "You can both sit in the den. Thanks for helping set the table."

Toby and Darcy walked out of the kitchen toward a burrow deep in Aunt Ellen's den. We trotted down the porch steps into the crisp night.

"Darcy's trying to do too much," muttered Margaret as she swung the door behind us. "I wonder if she shouldn't stop..." The door banged shut.

Shivering, I swiveled my ears back. Stop what? Working with me? That meant the farm. Pausing on the lawn, I listened, but the door blocked Margaret's words. I only heard the hum of her voice.

"It'll snow soon. You can smell it in the air." said Painter. He and Buster jogged into the dog run and lay down together.

I sat on the grass and stared at the big moon. When it disappeared, it would be time for the Dog Jamboree. I didn't want to think about it any more than I wanted to think of moving to a farm.

"Hey Belle!" Misty batted her favorite ball at me. It made jingling sounds when it bounced. "Let's play."

I let the noisy thing rattle down the grass. "I don't feel like playing."

"Why not?" She ran to the ball, tossed it high, and

pounced on it when it clattered to the ground.

"I'm bummed cuz I couldn't catch Bonehead. I'm so afraid he'll hurt Darcy again. And Toby. He's really turned out to be okay."

"Oh catnip." She flopped on her back and spun the ball with her front paws. "You can't mope about that. Try to nab Bonehead next time he comes around."

I supposed she was right, but it didn't make me feel better. "Herding dogs are supposed to protect the animals and people they love."

"You can't protect everyone all the time." She flung the ball at me again.

Bones. She'd pester me until I played. How like a cat, concerned only about herself and never anyone else. Catching the ball with my nose, I thrust it back at her. Maybe if I played rough, she'd leave me alone.

Stretching on her hind legs she flung it to me. "Come on, Belle. Play nice. I've been shut up in the house all day."

All right, I guess she had been. She may be a cat, but she deserved some fun, but we'd play by my rules this once.

"Ha! We dogs are always chasing you. You chase me for a change." Grabbing the ball, I spun and ran down the lawn toward the creek. If I crossed it she wouldn't follow.

"Come back here," she laughed, streaking after me.

I danced to the water, hurled myself onto the pile of leaves where I'd landed during agility practice, and dropped the ball. "Come get me. I dare you."

"No problem." She shot into the air and landed beside me.

Fleas! Snatching the ball, I sprang to the opposite bank.

She vaulted, ending up in front of me, and knocked the ball out of my mouth. It bounced to the poles blocking the foot path. We dove for it, but I grabbed it first, and dashed around the pole closest to the bank.

Dancing on her hind legs, she tapped my nose with velvet paws. "Give it to me."

I dodged and slithered around the pole in the middle of

the path, then circled the one closest to the trees.

Maybe I can hide this thing where she'll never find it. How about over...

Wait a minute! I didn't see Misty. Where had she gone? Could she have slipped into the creek? She had no front claws to grab anything. She'd drown.

Dropping the ball, I wheeled.

Misty sat by the pole closest to the water staring at me.

"What are you doing," I growled to hide my relief at seeing her.

Her tail twitched. "Belle. You just wove."

Now I gaped at her. "What?"

"You just did weave poles, all by yourself, without anybody steering you."

"I did not."

Her tail slashed the air. "You did. I swear it on a bag of cat nip."

Putting my nose to the ground, I traced the odor of my path around the poles. "Holy dog biscuits! You're right, Misty. How did I do that?"

"I don't know." Like a lightening bolt, she jumped and pounced on the ball.

"Hey, wait a minute." I sprang to grab it. Down as I was, no stupid feline was going to play a trick like that on me.

She pranced away. "Figure out what you did, and you get this back."

"You – cat!" I lunged at her.

She skittered around the pole closest to the trees, bouncing the ball ahead of her. I followed.

At the middle pole, she stopped.

I gave her a shove and herded her around the last barrier to the water.

She melted out of my reach, "Don't push me, doggie dog."

"I wove again," I said. "Give me the ball."

Sitting on it, she washed her whiskers. "Weave until I

tell you to stop."

I glared.

She met my gaze, eyes shining in the darkness.

"Misty, I hate you."

"You do not. Weave."

"All right. I love you as much as anyone could love a cat." I trotted around the poles.

"Faster," she taunted. "Faster."

I broke into a lope, then into a sprint.

She bounced the ball in the air. "Shake it, baby."

Dropping almost onto my belly, I circled as fast and tight as I could.

"You look like you're herding a cow," she laughed.

I felt like I was herding a cow. Of course. That's just what weave poles were like. Herding a cow!

I dashed around. And around again. The branches above me spun, and the first stars blurred in the black sky. My breath tore at my lungs, and my tongue felt like dry bark. But I was weaving. By dog heaven, I was weaving.

Finally I dropped to my haunches. "D-dog b-biscuits, Misty! I-I have to s-stop. Please let me."

She flicked the ball in the air. "Can you remember how you wove until the Dog Jamboree?"

"I'll remember how to weave forever. I don't know why I didn't figure it out before."

"I don't either, you funny dog. I would think it would be natural for you." Tossing the ball to me, she sprang to the pile of leaves at the far side of the creek. There, she turned. "Now don't forget, cuz I guess I love you about as much as anyone can love a mutt, and I want you to stay with Darcy."

In a bound I landed on the leaves and nuzzled her. "For once I'm glad you're a cat."

Chapter 10

Stumble

The moon shrank and disappeared. On the dark morning of Jamboree Day, Darcy woke me when she slipped out of her sleeping nest.

Holy bones, we didn't need to get up this early. Buster and I let out yips of protest.

"Shhh." Darcy put her fingers to her lips. "I need to finish a story for English, or I'm in trouble."

She tiptoed across her burrow and picked up a book. Then she glided back to her sleeping nest, pulled a long silver thing from under it and tossed the blanket over her head.

Click. Light shined under the blanket.

Laying my head on my paws, I wondered what the day would bring. One thing for sure, I could now handle weave poles.

After a while, a bird twittered, then another. A car rolled down the street. The burrow began to brighten, and soon gray light tinged with gold poured through the

73

window. Then I basked in yellow warmth.

Slipping from under the covers, Darcy read without the silver thing.

A buzz echoed in Margaret and Bob's sleeping burrow.

Buster rose. "They're up. It's time to go out."

I nuzzled Darcy, but she didn't look up.

"Woof." Buster pranced on his hind feet.

Steps tapped in the burrow hall.

Buster barked louder.

Darcy's door creaked.

With a start, she shoved the book under the covers and lay down.

"Hey, sleepy head, today's the big day," Margaret called, coming into the burrow.

Buster's wagging tail bumped Darcy's sleeping nest. The silver thing crashed to the floor.

Margaret stared at it. "Why are you sleeping with a flashlight?" Pulling back Darcy's covers, she spotted the book. "I thought your homework was done."

I could smell Darcy beginning to sweat.

Folding her arms, Margaret locked gazes with Darcy. "This is how you handle karate, 4-H, chorus, and school?" Margaret's voice took on an edge, and she began to smell like pepper.

Darcy sat straight up. "I-I didn't quite finish last night. I have two more sentences to go, and I'll be done."

Margaret didn't move. "This happened yesterday morning, too, didn't it, with math?"

Darcy's jaw dropped. "How did you know about that?"

"Mothers," said Margaret, "have eyes in the backs of their heads."

"Yeah." Darcy looked down at her hands.

Margaret picked up the silver thing and dropped it into the pocket of the outer fur she wore when she woke up. "I look at your notebooks now and then."

Darcy didn't lift her head. "I guess I'd better not let this happen again."

"I guess you're right." Margaret walked out of the burrow.

I put my head on Darcy's knee.

Letting out a long sigh, she stared at her hands. "She's right, Belle. Something's got to give. I can't do it all."

Ears lowered, I pushed against her leg. Please, don't give up on me.

She rubbed my ears. "I don't know what to let go."

Stroking my face, she opened her book, scanned the page, then snapped the book shut. "Hey, wait a minute. I do know how to manage everything. Come on dogs, let's go out. I'll tell Mom when she calms down."

What had she figured out? Ears flat against my head; I followed her down the hall, into the food burrow, and to back door.

A jumble of smells and a clatter of woofs engulfed me when Darcy led me through the door of the 4-H Building.

Mutts, Labradors, poodles, spaniels, and who knows who else bounced, scratched, jumped, and panted beside 4-Hers jamming the metal seats at the end of the arena.

Holy bones, I didn't know so many dogs could be alive.

Nostrils wiggling, I hunted for familiar odors. J. J.'s swelled, cheery, like frying bacon on a sunny morning. Then I caught a whiff of Cheri and sneezed. She must have had a bath with that stuff called soap. Painter's earthy aroma wafted from nearby. Beside me, Buster smelled like old, mellow wood.

Jumps, hoops, a dog walk, weave poles, tunnels, the A-frame and the teeter-totter gleamed in the bright light that poured into holes near the ceiling. The teeter-totter seemed to shine brightest of all.

What if I did bad on it? What if I forgot how to weave? Did it matter, if Darcy decided not to keep me?

A Great Dane's roaring bark shook the insides of my ears. How would I hear Darcy's commands with all this noise? I cowered against her.

She patted me. "It's okay Belle. This is just practice."

Why had I decided to dig out that day before the cold time came? I wouldn't be here if I'd just stayed put then.

Darcy led us to an open spot on the metal seats. Tucking my tail between my legs, I put my head on her lap.

Toby settled beside me with Painter. Buster flopped next to him and thumped his tail on the ground.

Margaret, Bob, Aunt Ellen and Uncle Jim sat with other grownups near the 4-Hers.

Painter touched his nose to mine. "Cheer up. This is going to be a hoot."

Yes, it might, because things can't get much worse. I tried to wag my tail, but only managed to make it twitch.

J. J. stood up and clapped her hands. "Okay everybody. The Jamboree is going to run just like a show. Each dog gets two attempts at an obstacle. A dog may not refuse an obstacle. If he does, he's disqualified and gets a white ribbon."

Darcy looked at Toby. "How can you be disqualified and still win a ribbon?"

"It's a cross between thanks-for-entering and third place. If you make it around the course but you're slow, you can also get a white ribbon."

Glancing at a tall skinny guy sitting at a table J. J. smiled. "Our judge here, Dr. Wilson, has set the course time at one minute. Go over that and you get a white ribbon. We begin with the dog walk, go to the tire, jump three fences, do the weave poles..."

I held my breath. Would she exclude the teeter-totter?

"...through the tunnel..."

"Remember to slide through on your belly," Painter said.

Buster lifted his ears to show he was listening.

"Thanks." I looked at him and Painter. "Keep your corners tight on the weave poles. Lower your front legs and kind of slide around them."

J. J. continued. "Don't go over the A-frame. It's a trap.

Go directly to the teeter-totter, and then to the table."

I thought I would barf.

The mock competition began. Some people kept their dogs on tabs. Others worked without them.

A shiver ran from my nose to my tail. If Darcy decided to take me off the tab, maybe I wouldn't know what to do on this unfamiliar course. On the other paw, running without a tab would be fun.

"Toby Johnson and Painter," called Dr. Wilson, after several dogs and their handlers had run. "Your turn."

Toby unsnapped Painter's tab and ran toward the starting line.

"Go," called Dr. Wilson.

Painter missed a contact point going up the dog walk, but got his paws right on the other side. He got both ends right on his second try. Then he rollicked over the jumps.

At the weave poles, he hunkered down and made his corners tight. When he finished he shot a glance at me and let his tongue loll.

Feeling warm all over, I wagged my tail hard. He'd learned from me.

Swish. Scratch. Painter slid through the tunnel.

Typical terrier. Too bad we couldn't just do the tricks we did best.

"Teeter-totter," Toby shouted as Painter emerged.

Drawing a deep breath, I let my shoulders relax, realizing I'd hear commands just fine.

Painter ran to the A-frame and began to climb.

"No, wrong," Toby dashed after him. "Teeter-totter."

Painter ignored the command. Some of the 4-Hers laughed.

"Painter!" Toby clapped his hands.

Painter needed my help. I stood to go to him.

"Belle, no." Darcy hung onto my leash.

Painter continued up the A-frame.

"Painter, that's a trap," I barked.

Toby clapped his hands. "Painter! Here."

Painter slid over the top of the obstacle.

He needed a reminder of where to go. Lowering my head, I slid out of my collar and loped toward the course.

"Stay, Buster," Darcy yelled and raced after me.

Painter looked at me bolting toward him, wheeled and ran down the dog walk to Toby.

"Belle, come." Darcy clapped her hands.

"Painter, teeter-totter," Toby ordered.

I walked back to Darcy.

Dr. Wilson gave Darcy and me each a stern look. "You're lucky she obeyed or you would have been disqualified for being out of control."

What a sour dog treat he was. Well no wonder. He loved to give everybody puppy shots.

Nodding to him Darcy put my collar on. "Bad dog," she breathed in my ear and marched me back to her seat.

"What did you go out there for, Belle?" Buster growled, giving me a disgusted glance. "Painter has to do the course himself."

I lifted my tail and rumbled back. "He needed someone to get him back on track."

"Sop trying to fix the world." Buster stuck his nose on mine.

"I can't help it. I'm a herding dog."

"You're also a trouble maker, ruining stuff for everybody else." His hackles rose. "Sometimes I wish you'd never come to live with us."

"Right now, I wish I hadn't either." Laying back my ears, I snarled.

"Belle! Buster!" Darcy wedged herself between us. "Cut it out."

We obeyed, glaring at each other.

Painter got off the teeter-totter with his paws in the right place and ran to the table.

"Down," ordered Toby, when Painter jumped on.

Painter stretched out, one paw dangling to the ground.

"Come." Toby brought Painter back to Dr. Wilson.

Dr. Wilson looked at a score sheet. "All right, young man. You did the jumps, tire, and tunnel perfectly. You have a major fault on the table because one of Painter's paws touched the ground. He also didn't make proper contact going onto the dog walk, and that's a major fault." He studied the sheet again. "He got another major fault for going off course. You lost about 30 seconds getting him back on. You'd get a white ribbon in a real show."

I held my breath waiting for Toby's temper to explode.

"Yes sir," Toby hunched his shoulders.

"Good try," said Dr. Wilson. "You might want to set up some traps and teach him to stay away from them."

"Yes, sir. Thank you, sir." Toby took Painter off the course. When he got back to his seat, he glanced at Uncle Jim and Aunt Ellen.

Uncle Jim smiled at him.

"We can do better, Painter," he whispered.

Buster let his tongue loll. "Toby's changed. I knew it."

"Darcy Simmons and Belle," called Dr. Wilson.

Darcy snapped off my leash and didn't put on the tab. With a sigh of both relief and reluctance, I walked to the starting line.

Dr. Wilson signaled us.

My heart began to pound as we jogged to the dog walk. Veering onto it, I plunked my paws in place on both ends, and we headed to the tire. I leapt through and roared over two of the jumps. My paws hit the third, but it didn't fall.

Rotten meat. Jumps were my best trick. How could I have missed one?

The chatter and barking swelled behind me, pounding in my ears. Shaking, I headed for the weave poles. My mind went blank. What was I supposed to do? Oh dog biscuits. Was Misty right? Did I forget how to weave?

Darcy pointed. "Weave."

An image of the creek, and the poles blocking the foot path formed in my mind. Of course. Like herding a cow.

I took off and wove.

"Perfect," Darcy called.

My head cleared. I love you Misty, and nuts to you.

"Tunnel," Darcy shouted.

I rollicked in, slipped and bounced off the wall.

Laughter swelled as I flopped from side to side. Dog biscuits. I struggled for balance.

"Belly!" Painter's muffled bark reached me.

That's right. Stupid me. Lowering my haunches, I steadied myself and slid toward the opening at the other end. When I popped out, the crowd roared so loud, I thought my ears would split.

"Teeter-totter," Darcy shouted

My tail dropped, and I froze in mid stride. I can't even jump right. How can I do the teeter-totter?

"Come on, Belle," Darcy coaxed.

Heart pounding, I sat down and refused to budge.

"You get two tries, remember," Dr. Wilson prompted.

Darcy repeated the command. "Teeter-totter."

Staying on my haunches, I pulled my lips back, and glowered.

The crowd guffawed.

Dr. Wilson gave Darcy and me a gawky grin. "Belle, you silly girl, why don't you want to go on the teeter-totter," he chuckled.

I mustered my most woebegone look.

"I'm afraid that's a disqualification," Dr. Wilson sighed as he looked at Darcy. "Which is too bad, because the other stuff she did was minor. You need to get her onto the dog walk and into the tunnel straight." He pushed his mop of blond hair out of his eyes. "She looks like a pretty good jumper. The occasional touch happens."

Nodding, Darcy looked at me. "Okay, Belle. We're spending some time on the teeter-totter." She started toward the pooch patrol stall. "Let's go."

Wait! We haven't finished the course. I glanced at the table.

"Wrong, Belle," Darcy clapped her hands. "We're

disqualified. We can't do anything else."

Couldn't I get something for doing the weave poles right? I tucked my tail between my legs as Cheri and J. J. trotted to the starting line.

"Get over it, Belle," Painter said when we got back to the straw bales. "I'm disappointed in you. What's your problem?"

"What's your problem with the A-frame," I retorted.

"I forgot to listen to Toby for a minute, that's all. There wasn't any reason for you to come herding me home."

I'd blown it again. "I'm sorry. It won't happen a second time," I said, but Painter had walked away.

No! Wait Painter! He was my friend, wasn't he?

"Watch Cheri, Belle," Buster called.

Forcing my attention back to the course, I saw Cheri sail through the tire.

"A-frame," J. J. shouted, pointing to the teeter-totter as Cheri landed.

I stiffened. The A-frame was a trap.

Cheri trotted toward the teeter totter, danced across pompom tail waving, and jumped onto the table.

"Down," said J. J.

Cheri dropped, eyes never leaving J. J.

"Come," called J. J. stepping off the course.

"Perfect run," called Dr. Wilson. "No faults. Not even minor ones."

A cheer erupted.

Dr. Wilson called over it. "Darcy Simmons and Buster."

I dropped my head onto my paws. I could never do what Cheri did. I couldn't even finish a class. Darcy was going to have to give me away. Bones. I'd miss her when I left. Sighing, I watched her and Buster enter the ring.

She made sure he went in a straight line to the dog walk. Lolloping across, he gallumphed over the jumps, and managed to keep his body low enough not to knock over weave poles. He swish-scratched through the tunnel on his belly, but not very fast.

Half way up the teeter-totter he stopped, lowered his head and sniffed.

"Come on, Buster," Darcy called.

He kept his nose on the board.

The crowd tittered.

"Buster," Darcy clapped her hands.

I drew a breath to bark him along, then remembered and shut my mouth.

Two or three steps at a time, Buster meandered.

The titters turned to chuckles, then to good natured roars.

The board came down, but Buster was so busy smelling that he didn't step off.

Darcy snapped her fingers in front of his face. "Buster, table."

Strolling off the teeter-totter, he wandered to the table, and flopped onto it, pulling his paws toward his chest at the last second.

"Two minutes on the course," laughed Dr. Wilson when Darcy and Buster finally walked up to him. "I'm afraid that, along with loitering on the teeter-totter, equals a disqualification."

Darcy and Buster returned to the Pooch Patrol stall.

"What was so interesting up there, Buster?" I nuzzled him.

"It smelled like a zillion turtles."

"Turtles?" I gaped. "How would turtles get on a teeter-totter?"

"That's what I was trying to figure out."

"All right," shouted J. J. "Let's break for lunch. "If you didn't bring your own, the First Baptist Church Youth Choir has sandwiches and cokes for sale."

Leading Painter on a leash, Toby touched Darcy's arm as she, Buster and I walked toward kids with big ice chests that smelled of human food.

"Hey, Darcy," Toby said. "Ellen gave me a sandwich, but would you stake me for a coke? I'll pay you back soon as I get my allowance again."

She looked at him. "What do you mean?"

"I forgot to take the garbage out last night." Toby looked at the ground. "So Jim took away my allowance for a week."

With a sigh, Darcy took a green paper out of her pocket and handed it t Toby. "I'm sorry. Sometimes Uncle Jim over reacts to stuff."

Looking up, I half-wagged my tail. Boy do you have that right.

"Aw, your uncle's okay. He's kind of like me. Except his folks were extra strict with him. Mine didn't care what I did." Toby stood up tall. "But if he could turn out okay, so can I."

Holy bones. Toby had changed.

Dr. Wilson strolled up, scratched my ears, and smiled at Darcy. "Keep working with Belle. Practice will teach her to discipline herself."

Darcy smiled her thanks.

That word discipline again. What did it mean? Sulking, I followed Darcy as she got her drink and came to join Margaret, Uncle Jim and Aunt Ellen by their metal seats.

Margaret exchanged a look with Darcy. "Both Belle and Buster need a lot more practice."

"I'll keep after them, Mom."

I looked at both of them. Did that mean I still had a chance to stay?

J. J. came to say hello. Cheri, Buster, Painter, and I rubbed noses.

"Cheri," I whispered. "Is discipline punishment?"

She wagged her pom-pom tail. "Sometimes. But it's also when you learn to do something so well that when something goes wrong, you fix it on the spot."

"Like when you got the wrong command?"

"That's right. She didn't realize what happened. I saved her."

"How did you know what to do?"

"By paying attention and watching other dogs who ran before me."

"Holy bones. You mean we're allowed to think beyond listening to commands and getting our paws in the right places when we do agility?"

The black poodle laughed. "You can't do agility if you don't think."

"But what about all the rules? Are they part of discipline?"

"Sometimes discipline means knowing what you can do within the rules." She glanced at the dog walk. "It doesn't matter which paw makes contact, just as long as one does."

My hackles lifted. "I did the weave poles right."

"Yes you did." She wagged her tail, "but you have to put together the whole package, Belle and do it right from the first obstacle to the last." Her eyes went to the teeter-totter. "Discipline can mean if an obstacle's on a course, you take it, if you want to or not."

I tossed my head. "Easy for you to say. I bet you like all the obstacles."

"Not the tire."

"What?" My breath caught in my throat and I stared at her.

Cheri shook herself. "I banged my head a couple of times, and it hurt worse than getting a face full of porcupine quills," she said. "Believe me. Discipline also means being careful."

"How did you make yourself jump through?"

"By remembering you couldn't swallow a bite of dog food by the time it takes to get that obstacle over with."

I stared at her. "So if I concentrated hard enough on what I was doing, I could finish an agility class?"

Cheri danced on her toes. "You could win an agility class."

"No!"

"You could beat me on three paws. You are smart and you are agile."

Holy bones. Darcy would be thrilled if I won an agility class. But could I really think fast enough to do it? And Darcy hadn't yet said how she would handle her homework problem. If she decided to drop agility and give me to a farm, why should I work hard in agility?

"I don't know, Cheri. Just getting through a class might be a win for me."

"Don't set your goals too low," she replied. "You don't know what you can do until you try to do it."

Chapter 11

Choices

"Concentrate," I told myself as Dr. Wilson showed us the afternoon's course.

He pointed to the teeter-totter. "We begin with this, then move to three jumps, then the A-frame…"

Okay, dog heaven. I looked at the roof. I won't be on that bone rattler for as long as it takes to eat a dog treat. I won't be on…

"…is a trap." Dr. Wilson's voice interrupted my thoughts.

I snapped my gaze back to the ring. A trap? What was a trap? He was standing between the A-frame and the tire. Must be one of the two. Bones! Why did I take my eyes off him? Why didn't I worry about the teeter when the time came to use it?

"After the trap, go to the dog walk and the weave poles," he instructed. "Then through the tunnel to the table." He walked to the platform and pointed beyond it. "The jump over there is the final obstacle."

I said the sequence back to myself and glanced at Darcy.

She sat on the ground, arms around her knees watching Dr. Wilson.

He picked up his list of dog handler teams.

Don't call us until I know where the trap is, please.

"Fir-r-r-rst up, Darcy Simmons and Belle," Dr. Wilson called.

My heart jumped and I thought I would barf as we walked to the starting line. The crowd's chatter swelled to a piercing buzz. I'd be mortified if I did bad and Darcy got upset with me.

"Teeter, three jumps, A-frame." I swallowed hard. Then what? Oh, Darcy, please know where the trap is.

She patted my head. "It's okay, girl."

Shivering, I ran my tongue over my chops and sniffed.

Her flowery odor enveloped me. "You can do this," she whispered.

If I didn't mess up, she wouldn't be angry. Glancing over my shoulder, I located Cheri. "Where's the trap? Please tell me."

"Listen to Darcy's commands, and you'll find it." She barked above the people noises.

Okay. I must concentrate. Drawing in and letting out a deep breath, I focused on Darcy. The spectator buzz turned back to laughter and talk. Dog biscuits, I loved her. I would do whatever it took to...

"Teeter-totter," she called.

My mind was wandering again. With a start, I snapped my head straight and jumped onto the course. Somehow, I found myself in the middle of the teeter.

"Missed the contact stripe," bellowed Dr. Wilson. "Ten

point deduction. Take your second try."

Rabid skunks. Tail between my legs, I hopped off the board and came back to Darcy.

"Concentrate," barked Cheri.

I climbed onto the teeter again getting my paws right and braced for the stomach-tilting drop.

Whoosh! Slam! The landing set me scrambling for solid ground.

"Contact," yelled Darcy.

I got a back foot on the stripe just before I leaped off.

"Jump," called Darcy.

Fine. Now I'd make up for the morning. Over the fences I sailed. The crowd whooped. I frolicked on my toes. Tire here I come. No, wait. The trap was around someplace. Swiveling my ears I listened for Darcy's voice.

"A-frame," she called from down the course.

The tire must be the trap. Good for me. I wheeled and doubled back to her. Now don't forget the A-frame's contact points, and get on straight.

Taking off like a bee heading from a flower to its hive, I reached the A-frame's ramp.

"Contact," Darcy called.

I plopped my front paws on the yellow stripes and bolted up. Heading down, I aimed for the stripe and hit it.

"Good girl." She praised, her flowery smell washing over me. "Dog walk."

I caught myself panting. This concentration stuff took effort. I was winded and my head ached. But the dog walk would be fun. I looked great on it.

"Contact," Darcy said as we neared the obstacle.

My breathing slowed, and my body relaxed. Head high, I hit the mark, strode up the ramp, and strutted.

Aunt Ellen's voice floated from the metal seats. "You're gorgeous, Belle."

The rest of the crowd cheered.

Smiling at them as if I were the Queen of the Pack, I paraded down.

"Contact," Darcy prompted.

I jumped to the ground, eyes still on the stands.

"Missed exit contact," shouted Dr. Wilson. "Ten point deduction. Second try."

The people groaned.

"Stupid dog," yelled Uncle Jim.

My hackles rose. You'll see who's stupid. Watch me on the rest of the course.

Without waiting for Darcy's command, I reran the dog walk, making sure I hit the stripes, then charged the weave poles.

"Belle," Darcy shouted. "Wait."

In no time, I finished the last pole and dived into the tunnel. The floor set me skidding and I dropped to my belly just in time to keep from falling.

The crowd whooped as I shot out the other end, stumbled and fell in a heap.

Darcy appeared. "Belle – "

Jumping up I shook, caught my breath, and galloped for the table.

"Belle!" A faint peppery smell wafted from her.

Oh-oh. I skidded to a stop. Wild again. *Con-cen-trate!*

"Table," she commanded, giving me a stern look.

Focusing, I hopped onto the low wooden platform and started to lie down.

Oh yes, tuck in my paws. Pulling my hind feet close to my body, I curled my fore legs under me. The image of Cheri watching J. J. snapped into my mind, and I locked my gaze on Darcy.

She watched Dr. Wilson.

"One, two. . . ." He chanted. "Three. Four. Five."

"Jump," Darcy said.

Exploding off the table, I pointed myself straight at the hurdle and skidded into take off.

"Slow down," Darcy called.

Too late. Hind paw clipping the bar, I half fell and half stumbled to the ground. The crowd moaned, then cheered as I kept my balance and the jump stood.

Rotten, rotten, meat! I slunk to the finish line, tail down, dropped to a sit and panted. Farm, here I come, I'm sure. Pressing my ears flat on my head, I waited to hear how bad I did.

Dr. Wilson stared down at me. "Two major faults for missing the contact zones." He looked at Darcy. "Her start was sloppy. She didn't get on the teeter straight. That's a minor fault."

I stared at the ground.

"On top of all that," he glanced at his score sheet, "she almost got away from you. If she hadn't finally stopped when you called her, I'd have had to disqualify her again."

Darcy sighed and nodded. "Okay."

His lips turned up. "She looked good on the jumps, the table, and the weave poles," he chuckled. "But if she doesn't manage to get the whole performance together, she'll tank at the real show this summer."

"I'll keep working with her. Thanks." Forcing a smile, Darcy led me out of the ring. "Come on girl. That was a little better than this morning."

Some improvement. We passed Cheri and J. J. on their way to the course. I glanced at the black poodle, but her gaze was locked on J. J. Lucky. She must think I was a real flea-brain. Heaving a sigh, I watched them take off.

Cheri rode the teeter, cleared the jumps and dodged the tire. Trying to do as well as they did would be like trying to fly. She and J. J. finished with the equivalent of a blue ribbon. What else would be expected?

When they left the course, Toby and Buster took a turn and managed a red ribbon. I felt so miserable, I couldn't muster much more than a tiny tail wag for their success.

"Buster and Darcy Simmons," called. Dr. Wilson.

I touched Buster's nose as Darcy stood up. "Do better than I did, for her, please."

"Do it yourself. Stop asking others to correct your mistakes," he snapped.

She led him to the starting line. He flew over the course tail waving. It smacked three weave poles into the air.

"Disqualified," called Dr. Wilson.

"Skunks," he muttered, not looking at me "One of these days I'll remember to carry my tail over my back."

"Yeah, next time," I growled.

Giving off a faint peppery smell, Darcy led him back to us. "What am I going to do with the two of you," she asked.

I made myself small at her side. Why didn't I listen to her on the course from the first obstacle to the last? Next time, by dog biscuits, I would, if I got a next time, that is. Cowering, I wished the afternoon to end.

When it finally did end, Margaret, Bob, Darcy, Buster and I drove in silence to Aunt Ellen's. Darcy and Margaret went into the food burrow. Painter, Buster and I lay on the porch.

Painter and Buster dozed, catching the last of the sun's warmth.

I lay, grateful for the rays on my weary flanks. I did not know when I'd felt so exhausted. Every bone in my body ached. I'd promised to do better on the next course, but I wasn't sure I wanted to see another one.

Finally as the sun sank behind the trees, I sighed in a voice only other dogs could hear. "I don't think I can do agility. I really don't."

Painter opened one eye. "Fleas," he retorted.

Head pounding, I stared at him. "What do you mean? You saw the mess I made."

"When you were paying attention to what you were doing, you were fine." He sat up. "Don't give me that 'I can't' stuff."

My hackles rose. "When wasn't I paying attention?" But I thought of the moment I glanced at the ceiling and missed identifying the trap, then the instant I turned to Cheri and lost command to run.

91

He gave me a disgusted look. "You know."

Yes, I did. The list went on and on. When I pranced on the dog walk and lapped up the crowd's response. When Uncle Jim called me a stupid dog and I got mad.

"All right, Painter," I sighed. "But concentrating with all those people around is hard. I'm not sure I can do it. Everything's a distraction."

"That's part of agility, Belle. You have to learn to ignore stuff."

"Why?"

"Because that's the game."

I sulked. "I don't even know if Darcy's going to keep me. It seems pointless to continue with agility."

Buster lifted his head off his paws and looked down his long nose at me. "Belle, sure as dog biscuits she won't keep you if you don't try to do it."

"What did you say?" Painter looked from me to Buster.

I stared at the porch floor.

Buster explained about Darcy and the homework and me and the hole under the fence.

Painter poked me with his muzzle. "Belle, you've got a rotten attitude."

"Me?" I shoved him back. "Why?"

"Because," snapped Painter, "you can't always do what you want to do when you feel like doing it."

"That's right," woofed Buster. "Sometimes you have to do what others would like."

I stuck my nose in his face and growled. "That's a case of the garbage can saying the skunk stinks."

"What do you mean?" Drawing back his lips, he exposed his teeth.

"You came alive the day you ran with Toby." I let him see my canines. "But you give Darcy just enough to get by. It may be more fun to run with a boy, but she's not one."

Buster's scruff rose. "Now just a minute!"

"You don't need agility, but she wants you to do it. Seems to me you need to pay attention to others yourself."

Letting out a snarl, he leaped to his feet. "You change your attitude or I'll change it for you."

A burst of anger washed away my weariness. I jumped up. "What did you say?"

He dropped his forelegs over my shoulders, flinging me to the ground. "Shut your mouth and do your best at agility. That's your only choice."

Shock waves rolled from my head to my tail. With a panicked yelp, I swung my head up. Clamping my mouth on his belly hair, I yanked.

He sprang backwards. I scrambled off the ground. Nose to nose, we stared each other down.

"Buster, I don't have any choice in whether Darcy keeps me or not."

"Dog piles you don't, Belle."

Painter jumped between us. "Stop!" he barked. "Break it up. Both of you."

We didn't budge. "You dogs be quiet!" Uncle Jim yelled from inside the den.

Painter butted me in the shoulder, then smacked Buster's chest. "Back off. Now!"

I staggered away from Buster, heart slamming against my ribs. He slid back on his haunches, panting.

Painter glared at us. Then, he fixed his gaze on me.

"Belle, wait for Darcy to make her decision before you assume you have no choices." Turning to Buster, he rumbled, "And you work harder on agility for Darcy."

Buster lowered his ears.

Painter glared at him, then faced me and waited.

I felt like a piece of rotten meat. Kind, gentle Buster was so mad, he was ready to bite me. "Fine, Painter, I'll do the stuff I don't like to do on the agility course, if Buster runs for Darcy."

Buster gave me a hard glance. "You mean it?"

"I mean it. I'd feel awful if you hated me."

He looked doubtful. "No one hates you, but will you believe she'll keep you, if you do your part?"

I drew a deep breath. "I'll try."

"Then I'll try harder for her." He offered me a tiny tail wag.

I returned it. "Okay."

Buster sighed. "I'm sorry I knocked you down, Belle. I shouldn't have lost my temper."

I kept wagging. "I shouldn't have asked you to do better on the course to make up for my goof. Forgive me, Buster please. You gave me a scare."

He touched his whiskers to my face. "I didn't mean exactly what I did. I got carried away. Let's start over."

Catching my breath, I gave myself a shake that rattled my collar. "It's a deal. And Buster, I love you. Maybe I needed a good scare."

"I love you, too, Belle." He gave himself an ear-flapping shake. "And I want to live with you. I'd be miserable if you left."

"I'll do my best to see that it doesn't happen." I turned to Painter. "This afternoon, I was goofing off. When I was focused I did do well."

"Keep your cool, Belle," he said. "Shut out the distractions. What would you do if you were herding cows in a noisy place?"

I thought "Keep my mind on them."

"So keep your mind on agility the same way. Pretend each obstacle is a cow."

Concentrate like I was herding cows. It's worth a try, I suppose. I touched my nose to his. "Thank you, Painter. I'll work on it. I'm sorry I tried to herd you today."

He nuzzled me back. "Forget it."

We pressed our faces together. Buster pushed his nose against ours, and we lay down in a clump, resting our heads on each other's flanks.

"Now if I could only catch Bonehead," I sighed. "Before he hurts Darcy."

"The human police can't even do that," Buster yawned. "Stop worrying about it. You don't even know he's after her."

I lifted my head. "No one will ever hurt her again if I can help it, Buster."

"I understand how you feel."

From the house, Darcy began to sing.

Closing my eyes, I listened to her sweet voice rising and falling and held back whimpers. How long would I be around to hear her? When she finished, I heard everybody clapping.

A shiver ran from my head to my tail, though I lay close to warm friends. What would she choose to give up? Surely not singing.

Painter lifted his head. "They must be finished with supper. Let's see if we can bark our way inside." Rising, he let out a bark that ended in a yelp.

I didn't want to go in. Suppose Darcy made her decision now and the news was bad for me? On the other paw, it probably didn't matter in whose den I discovered my fate. Sooner or later, I had to do it. Joining him at the door, I let out my best beggar's whine.

Buster moaned.

"You're going to give up what?" Staring at Darcy, Uncle Jim rattled his cup into the saucer. Coffee sloshed onto the table.

I cowered in a corner of Aunt Ellen's food burrow. She, Bob and Margaret sat quiet.

"Uncle Jim, please try to understand." Darcy lifted her hands and let them fall. "I've really enjoyed learning to sing this year. It's like – a whole new world for me – something I've never done before."

"But why give up karate, Darcy?" Uncle Jim looked bewildered. "You know girls need to learn self defense."

Toby stared at a plate of cookies in the middle of the table.

Darcy gave him a sympathetic look.

"She can come back to karate," Aunt Ellen reasoned.

"Let her focus on training Belle this year."

Drawing a deep breath, Darcy mustered her patience. "I can take karate next term for P. E. class. That way after I work with Belle every day, I can come home and study. I won't have to take extra time to go downtown to the dojo."

Uncle Jim scowled at me. "Why is a dog so important? Especially this stupid one."

"I love her." Darcy looked at me and smiled. "And she's not stupid." She glared at Uncle Jim.

"It's good to try something besides sports," said Bob. "Let Darcy explore music."

I walked across the food burrow and pressed against her leg.

Buster and Painter crowded close. Misty slid under the table and lay in front of me.

Uncle Jim looked from Bob to Aunt Ellen to Margaret.

"It's Darcy's choice," said Margaret. "Let her make it."

"But being in a karate class with a P. E. teacher and 30 kids isn't the same as taking private lessons from a master." Uncle Jim shook his head.

"I can go back to private lessons in the summer," Darcy answered.

"We're not trying to send her to high level competitions, Jim." Exasperation crept into Bob's voice. He smelled a little like pepper.

Uncle Jim looked at Aunt Ellen.

She dropped a hand over Darcy's.

"All right," Uncle Jim shrugged. "But it sure isn't what I'd do."

Aunt Ellen kissed him. "Not everybody has to do things the way you do, dear."

He looked at Darcy. "I suppose your aunt's right. You're old enough to choose some of the things you want to do."

"Thanks," she said, and pressed her lips to my ear, "I love you, Belle."

I rubbed my head against her hand. Thank you, dog heaven.

Buster pressed his face against mine. "You happy now?"

"Yes." I wagged my tail.

"You going to do your best at agility, even with the teeter-totter?"

"I'll try pretending it's a very stubborn cow and see where that gets me."

"Will you try for the very best ribbon you can get?" he persisted.

"I'll give it my best shot, Buster."

"Then so will I," He dropped a paw on top of my foot.

"Me too," said Painter. "We'll give the judge a contest to watch."

Misty flicked her tail. "You finally found your competitive streak, Belle. Don't lose it."

I looked at my friends. They always straightened me out when life got confusing. I was one lucky dog to have found them; and Darcy, Bob, Margaret, Aunt Ellen, and yes, probably Uncle Jim, and maybe even Toby.

Jumping up Buster danced around the food burrow. "There's going to be a contest. There's going to be a contest like nobody ever saw." He not only wagged his tail, he wagged his whole back end.

Painter and I joined him. Hopping on hind legs, we circled the table. Misty batted our faces with soft little paws.

Buster's behind slammed into the stove. A spoon clattered to the floor.

"Hey, that's enough." Uncle Jim clapped his hands.

We ran faster, skidding into each other.

Everyone began to laugh.

With a scowl, Uncle Jim opened the door. "Out!"

Sliding across the porch, we jumped down the stairs and headed toward the creek.

Painter lowered his nose to the grass, "I found a skunk trail."

"Don't follow it." Misty hopped onto a stump. "I don't want that stink on my fur."

"I smell last year's turtles." Buster reached the bank and dived into the water.

Painter snuffled into dry leaves. "Speaking of skunks, Bonehead's been here."

I sniffed. A barfy rotten-fruit stench drifted on a breeze.

"I bet he was lurking in the yard when we were at the jamboree," Painter muttered. "His trail smells recent."

Lowering my head I found his smell and followed it. "His tracks go almost to Aunt Ellen's garden. He's getting bold."

"Too bold for his own good," Painter rumbled, hackles rising. "Too bad none of us was here."

"I'd have taken his arm off." I blurted.

Misty scoffed. "You'd defend Toby?"

"I'd defend anybody against Bonehead."

"What if that put Darcy in danger?" She flicked her tail.

Darcy's laugh floated out of the human den.

Swiveling my ears, I listened to its gentle lightness. Stupid cat. She shouldn't have to ask.

Chapter 12

Disaster!

The moon grew, shrank and disappeared three times after the Dog Jamboree. I stood on Aunt Ellen's porch and sniffed a breeze that smelled of wild flowers, and fresh creek water.

Darcy and Toby rattled agility jumps, the dog walk, the A-frame, and – *sigh* – the teeter totter into position in fresh cut grass while Uncle Jim settled in a wicker chair with a cell phone and a newspaper.

Misty sauntered out of the bushes. "Who can run the course the fastest?"

We looked at each other.

She licked her whiskers. "I bet Painter. He's practiced hard with Toby."

Buster laughed. "I bet I can move pretty fast."

"I suppose so when you want to." Eyes turning to slits, she twitched her tail at me. "You couldn't win, Belle. You hate the teeter-totter too much."

Stupid cat! I lifted my chin. "Oh yeah? I'm going to try to win the 4-H agility show."

She stared at me. "Ha! That I've got to see."

I turned my back before I could snarl something I may regret. "Concentrate," I mumbled to myself.

Toby and Darcy came back to the porch.

"Let's make the tire a trap," suggested Darcy.

Dog biscuits. The tire came after jumps. I'd have to work hard to remember not to jump through it.

Nodding to her, Toby tapped his knee. "All right, Painter. Let's try it."

Uncle Jim lowered his newspaper. "Want me to time you?"

"Sure." Toby guided Painter to the grass near me.

Uncle Jim laid the paper aside. "On your mark, get set, go!"

Toby pointed straight ahead. "Jump."

Painter bounded over two fences and a box, turned toward the tire and paused, turned, and scrambled up the A-frame.

I recalled Cheri's comment about thinking on the course.

Toby pointed to the dog walk. Painter whipped across it, shot through the tunnel, and raced up the teeter-totter. When it clattered to the ground and he stepped off, Toby shouted for him to sit.

"Fifty-six seconds," called Uncle Jim.

Toby scratched Painter's ears.

Buster and Darcy tried next. Buster rollicked through the course and plopped onto his haunches as soon as he stood clear of the teeter-totter.

"Fifty eight seconds," called Uncle Jim.

"Told you Painter was going to win," Misty batted a leaf with her paw.

Joining Darcy at the starting spot, I ran my tongue over my lips to keep from showing Misty my teeth.

"Jump," Darcy said to me.

The wind sang in my ears, and the grass caressed my toes. Faster and faster I flew. Before I knew it, I dove through the tire.

"Belle, wrong. A-frame," Darcy called.

Misty rolled on her back, mewing with laughter. "You're gong to win, huh, Belle?"

Wheeling back to Darcy, I flew over the A-frame and dog walk, took a deep breath and headed for the teeter-totter. Somehow I got myself into the middle of it, climbed as high as I could, and closed my eyes.

Thud. Teeth rattling, I popped my lids open, and forced myself to look straight ahead. One paw barely brushing the contact zone as I hopped off.

"One minute and five seconds," said Uncle Jim.

I tucked my tail between my legs and glanced at Darcy.

Sighing, she looked at Toby. "I think I'm going to keep Belle on tab. She's just too wild. Maybe running off tab can be a goal for next year."

Toby shrugged. "It's perfectly legal to run tab your first show. Let's put the weave poles in. Tire's still the trap."

Darcy put me on the tab and we walked back to the starting line.

"Jump," she said, pointing at the fence.

The grass still felt good under my feet as I raced, but the flea bitten tab pushed against my throat. Ears and tail down, I loped, forcing myself to concentrate

"A frame," Darcy called.

With a long sigh I swung in its direction.

Painter and I each finished the course in fifty-five seconds, but he knocked over a weave pole, so I beat him, even though the teeter-totter shook my brain so hard I didn't look to see where I put my paws.

Still, I tossed my head at Misty. "So there."

She licked her whiskers. "Dumb luck. And Buster still has to run."

He beat us both, off tab.

It wasn't fair. He didn't need agility, and he was doing better at it than I. Tucking my tail between my legs, I sulked.

"Let's make the teeter-totter the trap," said Toby. "Run to the tunnel."

I could have licked him from head to toe. Darcy took my tab and we flew around the course.

"Fifty five seconds," Uncle Jim laughed. "What is she all of a sudden, part jet plane?"

"Beat that," I barked at Buster and Painter.

"We will," Painter shouted.

Buster gave it his best. By the time he dropped onto his belly into the tunnel a second time, his breath rasped and his sides heaved.

"Fifty six seconds," Uncle Jim called.

"Oh well." Buster shook and walked over to the big water bowl in Painter's pen.

"Okay, Painter," said Misty. "Show 'em both."

I held my breath as Painter and Toby took off down the lawn.

"Fifty five point five seconds," Uncle Jim said when they stopped.

I danced on my hind legs and barked.

Darcy laughed until I thought she'd have to sit down on the grass. "You silly dog. When I can keep your attention, you do wonders."

Painter nosed my ribs. "What's to bark about? You didn't win by much."

"A win's a win." I danced on my toes.

Painter snorted. "You need to learn to win gracefully."

Misty looked at me through narrowed eyes. "That's

right. Put the teeter-totter back and you're a goner. Don't be cocky."

"Maybe you're a sore loser, Painter." I growled. "And Misty, don't be so sure about the teeter-totter. I'll make myself manage it."

Darcy pulled my tab. "Sit Belle. Simmer down."

Sooner or later someone got mad when they lost a game.

Buster came out of the pen, water dripping off his chin. "One more will decide who's best."

I didn't want to play anymore, but I knew I had to.

"Let's use all the equipment this time," exclaimed Darcy. "Make it an endurance run."

Misty looked at me and laughed. "I wouldn't bet any catnip on you this time."

I gave her the blackest look I could.

Buster ran and knocked over a weave pole. I pranced beside Darcy until the teeter-totter, where I slowed down to make sure I got on right. When it dropped I made myself stay calm and step off.

"Fifty six seconds," said Uncle Jim when we finished.

"I can beat that," snorted Painter. "You moved like a turtle on the teeter-totter."

Ignoring him, I held my head and tail high. *You're lucky you're not lousy on some part of the course or I'd tell you about it.*

Painter and Toby moved to the starting spot.

Uncle Jim sent them off.

Painter's claws tak-taked over the A-frame, swished through the grass, and tapped across the dog walk, landing smack in the middle of the contact zone.

He roared toward the teeter-totter and shot to the top. Looking over his shoulder he barked. "That's how you do it, Belle…"

The board dropped. Staggering, he snapped his head forward, but the teeter slammed to the ground, hurling him off. With a yelp he landed on his front legs, staggered, and collapsed.

Memories of my tumble swirled through my mind. He must feel like he's been hit with a rock. Slipping my head out of my collar, I bolted to him. "Painter, are you all right?"

He tried to stand, then screeched, and crumpled into a heap.

"My paw," he howled. "My paw!"

"Wait," I said as Toby knelt beside him. "It took a while for my pain to go away when I fell off..."

"No, Belle," he whimpered. "I can't move my foot. I think I broke it." He closed his eyes and cowered.

Chapter 13

Standing In

Darcy and Uncle Jim ran to Painter. Toby stroked his head.

"I'm so sorry, Painter," I whimpered.

He looked at me, winced and closed his eyes. "This is my fault, Belle. I wasn't paying attention to what I was doing."

Because I was making you do it. I tucked my tail between my legs.

"We'd better take him to Dr. Wilson," said Uncle Jim.

Aunt Ellen appeared with a dish towel and tied it around Painter's jaw. "Safety muzzle," she whispered.

Uncle Jim hurried into the burrow where he kept the car and returned with a board. He and Aunt Ellen slid Painter onto it and carried him up the lawn. Toby followed.

Buster and I tried to go too, but Darcy grabbed our

collars. "Stay."

We dropped to our haunches.

She ran after the others.

They disappeared into the car burrow. The car's motor roared, moved into the street, and faded. Aunt Ellen's sweet aroma drifted into the food burrow. She must have decided to stay with us.

Tails between our legs, we slunk onto the porch. Misty came too. Aunt Ellen let us in.

"I was only teasing you guys," Misty said as we crept under the table. "I didn't want anybody to get hurt."

I sighed. "I started the whole mess by bragging I was going to win, and then carrying on like I'd invented flea collars when I beat Painter."

"Maybe we shouldn't worry about winning." Buster put his head on his paws. "Let's just all run the best race we can and be happy with that."

"No," I said. "Let's pay attention to how we go about trying to win. We can do it without getting in each other's faces."

Misty cuddled close to Buster and me. "Let's stop taunting each other." For once, she didn't lick her paws or whiskers like nothing happened.

I nuzzled her. Then we lay still.

Aunt Ellen filled our water bowls, but no one felt like drinking. She settled on the floor and we slid to her, putting our heads in her lap.

Tears tricked down her cheeks. As they spattered my nose, I licked her hand. Buster caressed her fingers with his whiskers, and Misty lay against her leg and purred.

After a long time, the car returned

Toby, Darcy, and Uncle Jim tiptoed into the food burrow. Lifting my head, I got a whiff of sadness on them like dead leaves, but smelled nothing of Painter. Holy dog biscuits, what had happened to him? Had he died? My heart pounded.

Toby peeled off his outer fur and tossed it on a chair.

"Painter broke his left foot," he sighed. "He's in the animal hospital tonight, and we'll miss the agility show."

"Oh no." Rising and putting her arms around Toby, Aunt Ellen looked at Uncle Jim. "The show's two months from now. Surely Painter's leg will heal by them."

"He'll be out of condition," Uncle Jim answered. "Dr. Wilson doesn't think he should run in competition until next year."

Aunt Ellen hugged Toby. "Of all the rotten luck."

Darcy put a hand on his shoulder. "I'm sorry."

He bit his lip and swallowed.

Feeling like yesterday's garbage, I brushed his hand with my nose.

He patted me, then sat down at the food burrow table.

Buster's ears hung low. "I wish there was something we could do."

Nobody answered.

I tried to picture Painter in a cage at the animal hospital. Was he in pain, or could he rest comfortably?

"Wait a minute," Buster said. "Maybe I could run agility with Toby."

Kind, kind Buster.

He walked to Toby, wagged his tail as hard as he could, and whimpered.

Aunt Ellen puckered her brow. "You can borrow a dog for 4-H agility, can't you, Toby?"

"I dono," Toby scratched Buster's ears.

"I think I read that when I looked at your dog project pamphlet," she persisted. "Go to your room and get it. Let's take a look."

"Hang up your jacket too." Uncle Jim glanced at the outer fur on the chair.

Typical Uncle Jim, telling people what to do no matter what was going on.

Toby picked up his outer fur and dragged into the back of the human den. Soon he returned with some papers. He and Aunt Ellen examined them.

"Yes, right there." She pointed. "You may borrow a dog, as long as you're the one training and caring for it."

Buster pawed at Toby's knee.

"Whose dog would I use?" Toby looked at Aunt Ellen.

Jumping on his hind legs, Buster stuck his nose in Toby's face.

Darcy pulled Buster to the ground. "You'd swear he's volunteering."

Buster cocked his head and gave her his best of-course-I-am look.

Aunt Ellen glanced at Uncle Jim.

He shrugged.

"Would you like to borrow Buster, Toby," Aunt Ellen asked.

"Sure." Toby brightened. "If it's all right with Darcy."

"Yeah," she said. "It's okay."

"I'll talk to Margaret," Aunt Ellen replied. "But Buster would probably have to come here to live, since you'd have to take care of him. That would mean two dogs when Painter comes home."

Uncle Jim frowned.

I lowered my ears. He would never live with two dogs.

Toby stood up straight. "I'd take care of both of 'em, sir, honest."

Darcy looked straight at Uncle Jim. Aunt Ellen folded her arms and stuck out her chin.

Uncle Jim laughed. "Looks like I need to learn to survive with two dogs."

Aunt Ellen and Darcy flung their arms around him.

I wagged my tail. The wonders of dog heaven never ceased.

Toby shook Uncle Jim's hand. "Thank you. I'll clean up the extra poop."

"You sure will," Uncle Jim replied. "Or Buster goes back home."

Then again, once Uncle Jim, always Uncle Jim.

Aunt Ellen picked up the phone. "I'll call Margaret right

now."

I turned to Buster. "If you come here to live, I'm going to miss you."

"Cheer up." He nuzzled me. "I won't be gone long. I think the moon will get big and disappear twice. Then it will be time for the competition."

I licked him. "I wish I hadn't gotten into that rivalry with Painter. He'd be okay, and you could stay home."

"Well, learn from what happened." Saliva dripped off Buster's tongue as he panted. "Don't brag and get others worked up. Just go about your business doing what you want to do."

"You're right, it's time to grow up and think before I bark."

He didn't answer. Instead, he listened to Aunt Ellen as she spoke into the phone.

I caught my breath and held it.

Darcy fidgeted on a chair. Toby jingled some money in his pocket.

At last, Aunt Ellen hung up and smiled at him. "Okay, Buster can stay here. Toby, go with Darcy and get his bed and food dish."

Toby gave Aunt Ellen a high five. "Great. Thanks."

Darcy fastened my leash to my collar. "Let's go, girl. Buster, stay."

I felt like something was ripping my heart out of my chest. Lowering my tail, I whimpered. "Watch out for Bonehead, Buster. Remember, keep low if you have a chance to corner him, or he could smash your ribs."

"I'll be careful, Belle, don't worry." Buster touched his nose to mine.

I pressed against his nostrils. "What will I do without you?"

"Learn to concentrate on agility," he replied. "Get ready for the show. Be happy that I can help Toby."

"Come on Belle," Darcy turned toward the food burrow door. "We'll work on the weave poles when we get home.

I'll let you try without a tab."

Without a tab! All right, I'd take Busters advice and work, show her I could concentrate.

As far as being happy for Toby, I wasn't sure I was quite ready to do that. Giving Buster a final lick, I let Darcy lead me outside.

She and I wove with and without a tab until we couldn't see in the glow of the sliver of a moon that rose at dusk.

"Good dog," she said, finally leading me into the food burrow.

The aroma of chicken skin lifted from the garbage pail beside the stove. My stomach growled. Between all the practice and excitement today, I was plenty hungry. If I moved fast maybe I could grab a bite...

A trace of Buster's odor wafted from someplace in the food burrow.

But I promised him I'd leave the garbage alone. Swallowing hard, I turned and thrust my nose into my water bowl.

From in front of the stove, Margaret laughed. "What's gotten into Belle? She ignored the waste basket."

Darcy poured kibble into my food bowl. "Maybe she's learning self discipline, Mom."

Self discipline? I'd just kept a promise. Unless – was self discipline part of doing what you said you would?

Margaret chuckled. "Belle, when you pay attention, you can do what you should."

Cheri had told me that, too. Concentrating and thinking did seem to work.

Buster's scent rose again from where his food bowl usually stood.

With a small whimper, I looked out the burrow window. The tiny moon hung just above a tree.

How can I wait long enough to see it grow big and disappear twice before we get through the agility competition and he comes home?

Chapter 14

Waiting

From under a tree in the back yard, I listened to the sound of Margaret's car fading as she drove Darcy to school. Bob had already gone to his office.

I sat with only the breeze and the sun for company. That yellow monster would creep across the sky, before it finally went down and I could go to Aunt Ellen's and practice with Buster. Rabid skunks, it would be a long day.

Ears low, I thought about trying to dig my way under the fence, even though Bob had reinforced it. Then I pictured Darcy grabbing my collar and glaring the way she did when Buster and I dug out and ran to Auntie Ellen's. I'd better find fun right here.

Thrusting my nose down, I sniffed for an idea. The grass smelled sweet, and I buried my face in it until its blades tickled my whiskers like cool fingers. That invited me to flop on my back and rub my fur against the ground.

As I rolled back and forth, my paw touched a stick. That might be okay to play with. Scrambling up, I tossed it high, then watched it land a couple of dog lengths away.

How far could I fling it? Giving the branch a whack, I sent it sailing half way to the human den. When it landed, I batted it onto the porch. It bounced off a chair and hit a flower pot. The rim rang.

Dog biscuits. Holding my breath, I prayed to dog heaven

the pot hadn't broken. The stick tumbled to the lawn. The pot remained whole.

I'd better not toss it onto the porch again. Sort of a rule, I suppose. Or was it common sense?

Could rules be common sense? Maybe. When you were on a leash, you walked by the side of the person holding you, so you didn't trip them. That was sensible.

But – what was sensible about stepping on a contact zone, or sitting on a table until someone called you?

Nothing.

I flipped the stick across the yard, then hunted something else to do.

The toilet plungers caught my attention. Weaving was work, and Darcy would give me plenty of that this afternoon. What about jumping?

Trotting down the yard, I turned and hurled myself toward poles. Over I soared. I raced as far up the lawn as I could, wheeled and bolted back at them.

Round and round I tore, jumping as high as possible. I didn't need the lift to clear the plungers, but arching through the air felt terrific. I sprang until my breath hurt my lungs and my mouth felt so dry I gagged. Gulping, I slid under the tree and drank from the bowl Darcy had left for me. When my mouth felt moist again, I glanced up.

Holy bones, no wonder I was panting! The sun had climbed past the middle of the sky. The breeze felt hot now.

Heading into the bushes, I located a shady spot and lay down. Playing games was a good way to make time go. Flopping onto my side, I nestled into the grass. On the other paw, so was a nap. With a contented sigh, I closed my eyes.

"Mom, look! Belle didn't mess up anything in the yard!" Darcy's voice woke me. Jumping up, I looked around.

She and Margaret stood on the porch. Long shadows snaked across the grass, spread up the steps, and touched their feet. The sun shone on the other side of the sky. I must have worn myself out and taken a long nap. Giving my head a collar rattling shake, I trotted toward them.

"Don't tell me you're calming down," Margaret laughed. Coming onto the lawn she scratched my ears.

Darcy clapped her hands. "Belle come."

I raced to her and sat.

"Look at that," she exclaimed. "I think she is calming down. Maybe we can open the doggie door again."

Margaret eyed me.

I lifted a paw. Please. I know how to keep out of trouble now.

Darcy pulled a leash from her pocket and snapped it onto my collar. "We have to give it a try sometime."

I wagged my whole back end. I'd gotten through a day alone. I'd be okay coming into the kitchen until Buster came home again.

"I don't know if I'm ready for opening the doggie door." Margaret frowned. "Let's see how she does in the yard for a while."

Rabid cats! Standing up, I put my ears back and gave her a sad look.

She chuckled.

All right, I wasn't going to get anywhere looking miserable. But somehow, I had to convince her I could behave inside. How could I do it? Maybe by trying as hard as I could to follow the agility rules, whether I understood the reasons for them or not?

Buster, Painter, Misty and I lay on Aunt Ellen's porch. Darcy and Toby sat on the steps sipping lemonade. Uncle Jim, Aunt Ellen, Margaret and Bob stretched on lounge chairs.

I looked at the moon hanging big, round, and white in the sky for the second time since Buster went to work with Toby and shivered from head to tail.

"Tomorrow's the big day," Uncle Jim looked from

Darcy to Toby. "You kids think the dogs are ready?"

"As long as Belle gets on the teeter-totter, I think we'll manage to stay in the class," Darcy replied. "She's really improved in the last month."

Margaret rubbed my ears "It's too bad she's still scared of that thing."

"Maybe they won't use it," Aunt Ellen suggested.

I gave dog heaven an imploring look.

"Don't count on it," replied Uncle Jim.

Darcy took a long sip, rattling the ice in her glass. "I'm not."

Then no one spoke. I wondered if I'd manage the teeter-totter. I wondered if everyone else wondered, too.

After a while, Toby shifted off the step to settle in the grass, facing the porch. "Know what I thinks' going to be cool tomorrow? A K-9 officer's doing an obedience demo during lunch."

Darcy leaned forward. "I read an article in the paper about that. They're doing a community outreach booth."

"Something to keep the younger brothers and sisters busy during the agility trials," laughed Uncle Jim. "I read that the officers work with a breed called a Belgian Malinois. I've never heard of it."

I let out a long sigh, guessing Uncle Jim hadn't heard of a lot of stuff. The humans chuckled with him, then fell silent.

Margaret and Darcy caressed my back.

I let my mind float, glad that both were pleased with me. Tomorrow would be thinking time. Dogs would bark and people would whoop as we raced the course. The arena would stink of hard working animals, and 4-Hers would crackle with excitement, like the air before a storm.

But right now, Darcy, Ellen and Margaret's flowery scents drifted around me. Toby, Bob and Uncle Jim smelled like spicy cookies fresh from the oven. Painter's terrier earth tang mixed with Misty's cat nip aroma, and Buster's sharp water plant odor.

I closed my eyes and laid my head against Darcy's hip. There was nothing under dog heaven like good friends nearby before the running got hard.

Then, down by the creek twigs snapped. Water splashed. I lifted my head.

Something smelled very strong. Bonehead? Nostrils flaring, I smelled long and hard.

"Raccoon," shouted Buster. Jumping up he took off bellowing.

Painter hobbled to his feet. The white bandage on his front leg glowed in the moonlight.

Toby grabbed his collar. "Stay boy. Dr. Wilson doesn't want you running."

Painter's tail dropped, and his ears fell back on his head.

Poor guy. I gave Misty a disgusted look, then turned and watched Buster dive into the bushes by the water.

The raccoon yipped, then dashed into the brush on the opposite bank. "Leave me alone. I didn't do nothin' to you," he screeched.

Buster plunged into the water and let it roll over his shoulders. Bubbles sparkled around him. With loud splashes, he headed for the opposite bank.

Toby clapped his hands. "Come back here. Darn it, I'm going to have to give you a bath in the morning."

Buster circled back toward our side of the water. Wallowing and scrambling he climbed onto land and dripped his way up the lawn. "I gave that guy a good run for his cache of winter food."

Misty jumped onto the porch railing. "Stay away from me."

Buster shook in her direction.

Growling, she sprang into the shrubs beside the house.

I came down to the lawn and touched Buster's nose. "Any sign of Bonehead?"

"Nope. Not even an old trail. Maybe he's left town."

I looked deep into the sky, beyond the moon. Let that be true.

But the sky just stretched, allowing the wind to set its clouds adrift.

Shivering, I lay my head between my outstretched front legs. What if Bonehead appeared tomorrow? I'd meet the challenge he presented, of course. But – what if that meant running out of the agility ring and getting disqualified? I'd lose Darcy trying to protect her. How could I take a risk like that?

On the other paw, the cops and a member of the K-9 corps would be there. If I could let them handle Bonehead, my obedience marks would be just fine.

Chapter 15

My Choice

I'll try my best to win this contest. I nuzzled Darcy as Margaret parked in front of the 4-H Building.

Darcy smelled excited – like the air before a storm. "I love you, Belle." Opening the car door, she took hold of my leash.

A shiver ran from my nose to my tail, and I touched my whiskers to her wrist. *I love you too, Darcy, and I'll prove it today.* Tail high, I jumped to the sidewalk.

Margaret led us into the 4-H Building.

Chatter and barks roared in my ears. *Holy fleas!* Every possible kind of dog was here, from Chihuahuas to wolf hounds. The show was going to be way bigger than the Jamboree. Heart pounding, I contemplated slipping my collar and running. Living on a farm would be better than screwing up today's trial in front of everyone.

Ha! *Some way to prove your love for Darcy, Fleabrain.*

The thump of feet startled me, and I spun toward the

sound. In one of the stalls at the edge of the arena, the police had set up their booth. At its center, kids raced in a circle around an officer.

"You're on fire," he shouted.

The kids stopped, dived to the dirt, rolled, and jumped up.

"What do you do if you catch on fire," the officer prompted.

"Stop, drop and roll," they chorused.

What a noisy game! My ears pounded, and I thought they would shatter.

Darcy pointed to a corner of the stall. "Hey, Mom, there's the Belgian Malinois and the K-9 officer. They're cool."

Following her gaze, I saw a dog resembling a German Shepherd, but with a lighter build. Head high and ears erect, he focused on the officer holding his sturdy leather leash.

I heaved a sigh of relief. If Bonehead came around, he wouldn't get away from that dog. I wouldn't have to make any tough choices today.

Darcy began to walk. I followed, but kept my eyes on the booth. In another corner, two cops sat at tables putting kids' fingers into black stuff, then onto what looked like the paper Darcy used for school. A third policeman took the children's' pictures.

By dog biscuits, with all the cops and their dog here, Bonehead wouldn't dare show up. What was I worried about? Spreading my nostrils and swiveling my ears, I focused on the sounds and odors of the agility trials.

Spicy boy smells cut through the air. They were familiar, and I spun in their direction.

Buster and Toby sat with other Pooch Patrol members on straw bales in a stall on the other side of the arena from the cop booth. Either side of Pooch Patrol, other 4-Hers and dogs waited for the contest to begin.

I strained on my leash, trying to get to Buster and the

comfort his gentleness would bring.

Margaret pointed toward the metal seats on the wall next to the stalls. "Aunt Ellen and Uncle Jim are in the bleachers with Painter. I'll go sit with them." She smiled at Darcy then stooped and patted my head. "Good luck, both of you."

"Thanks, Mom. See you later." Tightening her grip on my lead, Darcy guided me around a German Shepherd to the Pooch Patrol gang.

I touched noses with Buster, filling myself with his warm, water dog smell. "I'm nervous, are you?"

He laughed. "What's to be scared of? This is going to be a hoot. Look at the course. You'll love it."

I glanced at the arena. Jumps, a tire, a tunnel, a table, weave poles, a dog walk, and an A-frame filled it. The teeter-totter stood in a corner out of the way.

Dog heaven, thank you.

A roar erupted from the police booth. Children sat around a table with a telephone. "911 is not for fun," they shouted.

Fleas! The Jamboree had been as quiet as a sleeping burrow compared to this hullabaloo. How would I hear Darcy's commands when we ran? I glanced at the Belgian Malinois. He lay at his K-9 officer's feet, eyes open wide, ears swiveled toward the man.

If I had developed his level of concentration, I'd win this competition.

Something rumbled in the arena, and I jerked my head toward the new sound. Dr. Wilson's voice boomed into a little black stick. "Attention everyone, please line up at the judge's table to sign in."

I scrambled with Darcy to where he stood on the other side of the agility obstacles. There he placed a long stick against the shoulder of each dog that came by.

"Sixteen inches," he said when Cheri arrived. "You compete in the medium sized dog class."

Buster stepped up, slapping his tongue at Dr. Wilson's

119

hands.

"Eighteen inches. Go with Cheri." The vet gave him a playful push.

Where would I go? I was smaller than they. Tail lowered I stopped in front of Dr. Wilson.

"Fifteen inches," he said to Darcy. "You just make the medium division."

I'd be running with and against friends. I supposed that could be good or bad, depending on how the contest turned out.

"Time to go over the course," Dr Wilson boomed when he had assigned all the dogs to small, medium, or large groups. "Come walk after me."

We formed a line and he led us through the obstacles.

Ears high, I memorized their sequence: broad jump, tunnel, a couple of fences, dog walk, A-frame, another fence, the table and then the tire. Then a log jump, the weave poles and three fences close together.

"This course should take 50 seconds to run, tops," said Dr. Wilson when we finished. "When the dogs are performing, please hold down the noise."

I'd be able to hear Darcy's orders. I could have licked his face.

Dr. Wilson continued. "Dogs waiting to run must be under control. Any dog breaking loose will be disqualified." He cleared his throat. "Each dog and handler team starts the run with 200 points."

I leaned against Darcy and listened to him.

"Deductions will be given for faults and slow course times. 180 and up qualifies a team for a blue ribbon. 150 to 179 earns a red. Scores below 150 get a white ribbon. Now small dogs, get ready."

I used the small dog contest to burn the course sequence into my brain. Who won I couldn't say, but red and white ribbon winners left the course and blended into the crowd. Blue ribbon winners stayed at ring side, awaiting their championship round. It would come after lunch and the

K-9 cop performance.

"Medium size dogs, get ready," Dr. Wilson called.

A pre-storm excited smell exploded from Darcy's skin. "We can do it, Belle."

I jumped into her lap. Yes we can.

Then I caught a different odor, sour, fruity and peppery, from the bleachers. My nostrils flared. Bonehead? Despite the cops? It couldn't be!

Dr. Wilson spoke. "First medium size dog up, Cheri and her handler J. J. Rogers."

Cheri walked off tab to the starting line.

J. J. pointed ahead of her, "Broad jump," she called.

Turning into a black streak, Cheri arched high over the jump, and dove into the tunnel. She wove the poles and stopped at the table, while the crowd murmured appreciation of her elegance. When she sailed over the last three jumps and dropped to a sit at the finish line, applause burst.

"Atta way, J. J," Toby bellowed.

"Forty-nine and two-tenths seconds," called Dr. Wilson. "Two minor faults. You didn't get onto the A-frame straight, and you veered left to the next obstacle when you got off. That's a deduction of 8 points. A blue ribbon run. J. J. and Cheri will contend for the county championship in their class this afternoon, and a chance to compete in the state 4-H agility show."

Cheri jumped up and kissed her mistress as J. J. took the ribbon. The electric smell on Darcy grew stronger.

Then the sour, peppery, and this time unmistakable stench of Bonehead overpowered me. I could hardly believe what I was smelling, but it was real. I let out a thunderous bark. "Bonehead! He's here."

"Belle!" Darcy grabbed my collar. "Quiet. Sit."

A growl rolled in my throat. Straining against her grip, I tired to look around.

"Where is he?" Painter roared back from the bleachers.

"Somewhere behind you." Buster shouted right beside

me. "Turn around, Painter."

"Buster and Toby Johnson up next," Dr. Wilson called.

Toby snapped a tab on Buster's collar. "Come on boy. Let's go."

Buster looked over his shoulder at me. "Help Painter, Belle."

My heart did a double flip. "I'll get the cops' attention, Buster! Run a good race." One eye on Painter, I watched Buster and Toby approach the course.

The hair on Painter's back stood up. "Bonehead's on the very top row."

I wheeled, focused my gaze on the police dog, still at the K-9 officer's feet, and barked as loud as I could. "Help! Look up the bleachers at the guy who stinks like rotten fruit. He's dangerous."

The Belgian Malinois glanced at me, then toward the seats. His nostrils flared. "Phew. You're right," he said in a voice only a dog could hear. "He smells like lots of stuff that makes cops go after people." He nudged his handler's leg. Turning, the cop scanned the crowd, and stared at Bonehead.

Painter wrenched out of his collar. Stiff, but still quick, he scrambled up the bleachers.

Uncle Jim clambered behind him. "Come back here."

Bonehead sat in the middle of the top row, eyes watching Toby.

"Belle, come help me," Painter barked.

I shouted at the police dog. "Get that man."

"I can't, unless Officer Rutherford tells me to," he answered, glancing at his handler.

Snarling, I glared at Officer Rutherford. "Order him to go after Bonehead, you flea brain."

The cop Rutherford didn't move. He just kept watching Bonehead.

All right, I'll make you give the command. Twisting, I tried to wrench my head out of my collar.

Darcy flung her arms around me. "Belle, calm down."

"Trust us. It's okay," the Belgian Malinois said. "If this guy's a problem, we'll take care of him."

I smelled Darcy; peppery, stormy, and flowery all at once. I had no choice but to trust Rutherford and his Belgian Malinois I supposed. *Dog heaven, make them be right.*

A murmur arose. Feeling helpless, I glanced at the arena.

Tail arched over his back, Buster skimmed through the weave poles. Toby jogged beside him.

I turned my attention back to the bleachers. Uncle Jim grabbed at Painter and missed. Aunt Ellen and Margaret watched Toby.

Aunt Ellen cheered. Turning again, I saw Toby and Buster complete the last jump. Buster dropped to his haunches at the finish line, sides heaving and tongue flopping.

"Forty eight seconds," called Dr. Wilson. "A four point deduction for touching a jump with one paw. But still plenty of points for a blue ribbon. Another team in the championship round."

Buster beat Cheri! Holy bones. I could out run him. A quiver ran down my back.

Toby took his blue ribbon from Dr. Wilson and came back to us, Buster bouncing beside him.

Darcy let me go and she and J. J. pounded Toby's back. I gave Buster a smooch on the nose.

Then in the bleachers, a yelp echoed.

Painter! He sounded hurt! I wheeled around.

Painter's paws clung to the foot rest under the top row of seats, head sticking above the metal slat.

Uncle Jim stretched his arms to grab him.

Bonehead stomped on Painter's feet. Painter fell with a screech.

Ready to run, but forcing myself to stand still, I looked at Officer Rutherford. He was beckoning to the other cops in the booth.

Uncle Jim sprang at Bonehead.

Bonehead catapulted around him and raced down the rows of seats. As he drew near Aunt Ellen and Margaret, they hopped out of his way, then ran after him.

Landing in the arena, Bonehead dashed into our stall and grabbed Toby.

Dogs and people scattered. Three of the police who were working with the kids charged out of the booth. The last one stayed with the children. Officer Rutherford guided the Belgian Malinois into the arena and waited. Both he and the dog focused on Bonehead.

"Come on, Toby," Bonehead shouted. "We're getting out of here."

"No way," Toby twisted in his grasp.

Snarling, Buster lunged between Bonehead's legs and grabbed his pants.

Bonehead kicked Buster's ribs.

Buster screamed, tumbling backwards.

"Go away," Toby yelled, trying to push Bonehead. "Go back to jail."

Bonehead gripped both Toby's arms. "You don't tell me to go away. I'm your father."

The three cops reached Toby and Bonehead. One grabbed Toby; the others Bonehead.

The crowd gasped.

I bellowed at the police dog. "Why won't Rutherford let you go?"

"He'll call me only if that man can't be contained any other way. In this crowd, I could accidentally hurt someone else if they stumbled into my path. Just be patient."

Dr. Wilson spoke into his black stick. "Ladies and Gentlemen, stay in your seats. 4-Hers stay in your places," His voice shook, and the sick stench of fear rolled off him. Gulping, he cleared his throat and took a deep breath. The aroma of strength rose above the terror, like a hundred drenched oaks standing up to a storm. The panic churned beneath it, as if Dr. Wilson held it down by force.

"Pooch Patrol, you come to the middle of the arena.

Quickly. Quietly," he directed in a firm and urgent tone.

We rose and fanned out of the stall, avoiding the cops. Dr. Wilson beckoned us to his table.

With a violent twist and two hard kicks, Bonehead knocked down the officers holding him. Wrenching Toby from the third cop, he dashed toward the exit.

"Stop," yelled Officer Rutherford. "Hit the ground, or I'll turn the dog loose. This is a warning."

Thank you dog heaven.

Uncle Jim jumped down the bleachers and sprinted after Bonehead, followed by the cop who'd held Toby. The other two scrambled to their feet and joined the chase.

"Darcy, Come here," Margaret called from near Dr. Wilson's table.

Darcy gripped my leash and pulled me toward her, blundering into Bonehead's path.

His shoulder slammed into hers, knocking her off balance. Foot twisting, she crumpled into the dirt.

All right, that's enough. I wrenched free of my collar and charged at Bonehead's feet. His boot shot at me. Dropping to my stomach, I skidded aside, and slid between him and Darcy.

Buster appeared, teeth bared.

"Block his way out," I roared, then butted my head into Bonehead's knee, driving him toward the bleachers.

A white blur shot from under the lowest seats, and Painter planted himself opposite me.

"Close in," I screamed. "Force him into the stall."

They swarmed in snapping at Bonehead's boots and pant legs. Toby pulled away from him and fled

One cop dashed up to him. The others ran after us.

Arms waving, Bonehead staggered backwards.

"Keep him moving," I bellowed.

Bonehead stumbled into the stall, tripped on a bale, and sprawled.

As we lined up in the stall door and barked, I smelled Aunt Ellen and Uncle Jim's scents mingling with Toby's.

The police grabbed Bonehead. Writhing, he half-rose, trying to pull away.

"On the ground," Officer Rutherford bellowed. "I have a dog."

The Belgian Malinois stared Bonehead down, and crouched to spring, should his handler give the command.

Bonehead looked at the animal's jaws, and lay face down on the ground. Two cops fastened his hands behind his back with some kind of metal leash, then pulled him to his feet and gripped his arms.

The Belgian Malinois looked at me. "Well done. You organized a capture as well as I could. What's your name?"

"Belle," I panted.

"I'm King," he said.

Dr. Wilson hurried to us, a frown darkening his face. "Belle, Painter, and Buster. What are we going to do with you?" Peppery anger mixed with his smells of fear and strength.

Rabid skunks. Should I bask in King's praise, or dig a hole in the arena and burrow into it? Here came disqualification I was sure, for both me and Buster. Dog heaven, help Margaret to know I was defending Darcy. Don't let her send me away.

Darcy scrambled out of the dirt. Hopping on one foot, she pointed to Bonehead. "H-he's a convict, escaped from prison."

Margaret appeared and put her arms around Darcy.

Darcy slithered away from her and limped to Dr. Wilson. "Don't disqualify Belle and Buster, please." Her voice shook as she struggled to catch her breath.

Margaret followed her, one hand outstretched. "Honey..."

Bonehead glowered at his captors. "You've got the wrong man. I'm not Fred Johnson. My name's Sam Miller."

"Bunk," Toby shouted as he, Uncle Jim, Aunt Ellen, and their cop moved toward us.

Taking Toby by the arm, Uncle Jim shook his head.

One of the officers gripping Bonehead laughed. "I've picked you up before, Mr. Johnson. If you're Sam Miller. I'm Santa Claus."

I looked at King. "As if changing his name's going to let him escape."

The police dog lifted his chin. "To call people like him flea brains would sometimes be an insult to fleas."

Darcy faced Dr. Wilson. "Buster and Belle weren't out of control. They were protecting us."

She turned to Margaret. "Mom, Belle did the right thing, even though it looked wrong."

The other cop holding Bonehead laughed. "That's putting it mildly. She caught a man who's dodged us for months." He gave Bonehead a disgusted look. "Fred Johnson has been missed at the state pen."

King waved his tail at me. "See? You've got real leadership potential."

My ears sagged and I looked at the ground. I should have danced on my toes at such praise from a dog with an important job. But what good were compliments if I lost Darcy? Holy bones, I should have let the cops do the job of catching Bonehead.

Something rustled in the police booth. Glancing up, I saw the officer who had stayed with the children herding them to their parents. When the last one had gone, he jogged over to us.

I caught a familiar scent on him, but couldn't place where I'd smelled him.

Dr. Wilson sighed and looked at Darcy. "How can I not disqualify Buster and Belle? They broke the agility rules when they ran loose." The stench of fear had gone from him, leaving the smells of peppers and drenched trees that were beginning to dry out.

The officer from the booth spoke. "Excuse me, Dr. Wilson. I think I understand what's happened here." Drawing Dr. Wilson aside, he spoke in a low voice.

I took a good long sniff of the cop. By dog biscuits.

He was the one who took Toby and Bonehead away last summer for beating up on Darcy. He knew us. I looked up at Darcy with a hopeful tail wag.

A tear trickled down her cheek. "Oh, Belle. I know you're a good dog."

Margaret put one arm around her.

After that, nobody moved. Cuddling close to Painter and Buster, I watched Dr. Wilson with his cop, then shifted my gaze to the cop talking to Uncle Jim, Aunt Ellen, and Toby.

What would happen to me when they finished their discussions? Maybe I'd better say good-bye to Darcy now. I touched her wrist with my whiskers.

Enough time seemed to pass for the moon to grow big, small and disappear, but finally Dr. Wilson nodded and stepped away from his policeman. Toby and Uncle Jim left theirs.

All the cops save Officer Rutherford and King gathered around Bonehead and started for the exit.

Uncle Jim, Toby, and Dr. Wilson rejoined us.

Buster, Painter, and I sucked in our breaths.

Squatting on his heels, Dr. Wilson petted me. "Belle, you're a remarkable little dog." Rising, he smiled at Darcy and Margaret. "The cops told me all about your escapade with Fred Johnson last year."

Darcy waited.

"I think," said Dr. Wilson, "under the circumstances we're going to allow Belle to remain in the class. And Buster, too."

Her breath came out in a burst. "Thank you."

I could hear the thankfulness in her voice, and believe me, I was plenty thankful, too. I wagged my tail as hard as I could, and Buster danced on his hind legs.

Toby grabbed Buster and offered him a shaky smile. "On to the championship round, boy. My dumb dad is not going to stop us."

"That's the spirit." Uncle Jim thumped Toby's shoulder.

Darcy looked at Margaret. "Can Belle and I continue, Mom? Please?"

Margaret shrugged. "If Dr. Wilson's happy, I'm happy. But can you walk? Your ankle looks like it's swelling."

Darcy took a hobbling step. "It hurts, but I think I can run with Belle."

"I wonder," said Margaret, keeping a hand on her arm.

Dr. Wilson bent and studied Darcy's feet, then ran a finger over her ankle.

She grimaced.

"You sprained it, Darcy," he said. "I don't think you should be running. Could you take Belle off tab and walk behind her calling commands?"

Darcy looked down at me. "I – I don't know."

"You've done it at home," said Margaret.

Toby nodded. "And she does okay most of the time. When she forgets to pay attention is when you get in trouble."

"That's what I'm afraid of. What if she messes up?"

"Then she goes to a new home, just as she would have on the tab," Margaret replied.

"If I choose not to run her, could I try again next year?"

"No, Darcy. You have to take the chance you've got, even if it's not the best."

Darcy looked down at me. "All right. We'll do it. Belle, the outcome's up to you."

My heart turned to fire and my stomach to ice.

Chapter 16

Giving It My All

"Now up, the team of Darcy Simmons and Belle," called Dr. Wilson.

We walked to the starting line. Beyond it, the obstacles shimmered as if I saw them in a dream. Heart pounding, I reviewed the course. Broad jump, tunnel, dog walk and the A-frame. Keep my paws on the table when I lie down.

Applause swelled as Darcy positioned me in front of the broad jump and took off my tab.

Out of the corner of my eye, I spotted King and Officer Rutherford watching me. "Go for the Blue," King said in the voice that only a dog can hear.

"You can do it, Belle," Painter woofed.

Could I? Totally without Darcy? The arena blurred, and I squeezed my eyes shut.

"Concentrate," called Cheri.

I opened my eyes. The course swam into focus. A map formed in my mind.

All right. If an agility expert and a police dog think I'm capable, maybe I am. Looking from King to Cheri, I wagged my tail.

"Ready girl," Darcy asked.

I cocked my head, and fastened my gaze on her.

She took a deep breath and stepped over the starting line. "Broad jump."

I sailed over it and dove at the tunnel before I thought about it. As I popped out of the other side, I saw her hobbling toward me.

"Jumps, girl." She cut across the arena to the dog walk.

Yes, and then, don't forget the dog walk.

One, two, three, I cleared the jumps. Darcy pointed straight at the dog walk. Planting one paw in the contact zone, I raced up and crossed.

"Good job," Buster bellowed. "Keep that concentration."

"A-frame," shouted Darcy.

Elation swept from my nose to my tail. Gathering my strength, I sprang onto the slanted plank.

"Fault," shouted Dr. Wilson. "Missed the contact zone."

His voice hit like a slap on the nose. How could I have forgotten to step into the yellow stripe? Stupid me. No, keep focused.

"A-frame, Belle," said Darcy. "Try again."

I watched my front paw hit the proper spot. Gulping air, I tore up the ramp and all but slid down the other side. Both fore feet hit the contact zone.

Bones, why couldn't I have done that the first time?

Catching Darcy's scent, I looked up to see her pointing at the next jump. Ears cocked for another command, I sailed over.

"Table," she called.

I vaulted onto it. She hobbled around in front of me. I locked my eyes and ears on her.

"One, two…" Dr. Wilson counted.

My paws! Where had I placed my paws? With a gasp, I looked around. Thank you, dog heaven. I lay in the middle of the table. No legs dangled.

"...three, four, five," Dr. Wilson finished.

"Belle, come," Darcy called.

Catching my breath, I sprang through the tire, but as I came down my hind paw hit the rim.

Dog piles! With a snarl, I catapulted over the log jump.

Weave poles came next. I pranced around each. Well, maybe Misty could at least be proud of me. Then I sprang high over the three jumps, slid to the finish line and sat.

Darcy limped up and scooped me into her arms. "Good dog."

Good dog? Did she have fleas in her brain? Couldn't she see I'd made a mess of the run.

"Fifty eight seconds. Five point deduction for missing the contact point on the A-frame," called Dr. Wilson. "Three points off for hitting the tire jump, and one point off for each second over time. That just puts Belle into the blue ribbon category."

The crowd clapped, though not as loud as they had for Buster and Cheri.

Sliding out of Darcy's arms, I tucked my tail between my legs. She led me out of the ring.

"Way to go, Darcy," Uncle Jim bellowed.

Aunt Ellen and Margaret cheered. Painter woofed a congratulations.

Head down, I crept past the bleachers, unable to look at anyone. Why were they fussing over me? They ought to be furious.

Cheri met us at the stall door. "You bounced off that mistake, good job."

"How do you figure?" I flopped down on the dirt and sighed.

"You didn't let it throw you. You kept going. That's what you need to do. You still have a chance at the purple ribbon."

Maybe, but what if I screwed up again? Sighing, I ran my tongue over my chops and stole a glance at King. I'd sure proved him wrong.

He flicked his tail. "Just keep at it."

Buster came over. "You looked great out there, other than missing the contact point."

"Mistakes happen," said Cheri. "The first year I tried for the state championship, I lost my footing and knocked down the first jump."

"Put it behind you," said Buster. "When you run in the final round, it's a new chance."

I looked at Cheri. "What happens in the second round?"

"The dog who finishes closest to time with the least number of faults wins a purple ribbon. The dog that finishes next best gets a red, white, and blue ribbon. Both go to state trails and compete there."

"And the dogs who don't win one of these ribbons – are they disqualified?"

"Not unless they refuse an obstacle."

I glanced at the teeter totter in its corner. "You think they'll put that thing in next round?"

"I'm sure of it."

"Oh dog biscuits." I swallowed the urge to run for the exit.

"Come on, Belle," Buster lifted his chin. "You can go the distance."

I wasn't so sure.

Chapter 17

Facing the Trial

Buster, Cheri, and I stood in a circle with Toby, J. J. and Darcy.

The tilt of Cheri's head told me she wanted to win and go to state trials for the third time.

Buster lifted his head, ready to tear down the course when Toby said the word.

I shoved my nose under Darcy's hand and pushed hard against her leg. "I'll do my best and hope it's enough."

"Good luck," J. J. held her hand out to Toby.

Everyone shook hands. We dogs touched noses.

"Have a good run, Buster," I said. "You too, Cheri."

We walked the course. When I got to the teeter-totter, its fall rattled my spine. My legs shook as I stumbled off and I nicked the cross bar of the jump that came next.

When we got back to the Pooch Patrol stall, Darcy stroked my head. "It's okay, girl," she whispered. "I'd like to win, but – you know, it's fine if we don't."

I'll try, Darcy. I'll try. I took a long look at the course. Start with the dog walk. Next left to two jumps. Don't go straight to the tire. That's a trap. Turn right to the tunnel...

"Let's begin," said Dr. Wilson. "First up Buster and his handler, Toby Johnson. This course, by the way, should take no more than one minute to complete."

Head high, Buster walked to the starting line with Toby.

I gasped as light dappled his black coat. "You're magnificent! Go for it."

He trotted up the dog walk, tail waving.

"Fault," Dr. Wilson yelled. "Missed contact."

Oh Buster.

Ears dropping, he followed Toby back to the beginning of the course to take his second try.

This time he hit the mark and raced over the dog walk, cleared the two jumps, turned for the tunnel and half-slid and half-wallowed through it.

The crowd chuckled, but Buster made it out fast, and Toby turned him away from the tire.

Before I could take three breaths and let them out, Buster sailed over the broad jump, scrambled up and down the A-frame, wove the poles, and flopped panting onto the table.

Don't let your paws slide off.

They stayed on. Dr. Wilson counted five.

Toby sent Buster to the teeter-totter. When it fell he galloped toward the last jumps. But his sides heaved, and his tail hung limp.

"Come on boy, keep going," Toby coaxed.

Buster managed the last three leaps and dropped to a sit at the finish line.

"One minute. Five point deduction for a major fault."

The crowd clapped. Toby brought Buster back to us and filled a water bowl for him.

"Holy bones, Buster. Now you ran a race," I said.

"I-I-I had t-t-time to – to make up a-after that m-mistake." Catching his breath, he plunged his nose into the bowl.

If I messed up a contact zone and the teeter-totter... No, I would remember the contact zones and focus hard on the teeter totter.

Buster shook water off his mouth. "It's an exhausting course."

What if I got tired and lost my concentration and knocked down jumps? No! I'll find the strength I need somehow.

Cheri and J. J. ran, and completed the course in 59 seconds, with one minor fault putting them in first place over Buster.

Those two are going to be hard to beat.

Darcy rose. "Okay, Belle, it's our turn. You're a good dog. I love you."

She smelled like electricity, and I could hear her heart pounding. My own thumped as I walked to the starting line. One last time I repeated instructions to myself. Remember the tire trap and don't forget the contact zones.

I felt a tug at my collar as Darcy removed my tab.

"Get ready, girl," she whispered.

The course blurred. Forcing my mind clear, I focused on the dog walk.

"Go," commanded Darcy.

I took off, planted a paw in the contact zone and raced up the dog walk.

"You look great," Buster barked.

"Gorgeous," Painter agreed.

"Keep it up," called King in a voice only a dog could hear.

Their encouragement bolstered me. Strength welling in all my muscles, I pranced off the dog walk, plopping a paw on the yellow stripe before I stepped to the ground.

Darcy moved behind me as fast as she dared. "Good dog, Belle, jump."

I flew over both fences.

"Tire," commanded Darcy.

No! The tire's a trap. I turned hard to the left toward the tunnel.

"Good dog. My mistake," Darcy praised.

I'd gotten her out of a jam. Energy shot through me, and I dived into the tunnel, but when I emerged she wasn't there to meet me. Tail drooping, I looked around. What did this mean?

Then I saw her, hopping toward me on one foot

"She twisted her ankle again," woofed Buster.

No way could she stay near me now. If I finished the course, I'd do it alone. My heart did a double flip. When I ran without a tab in the yard, Darcy always stayed very close to me. Now what would I do? Holy dog biscuits, which obstacle came next?

"Broad jump," Darcy panted, hobbling to the center of the course.

All right. I can do this. Taking a deep breath, I sped to the broad jump and leaped.

The A-frame would be next. Remember to get on straight.

"Contact," Darcy called.

My paw plopped onto the yellow stripe. I scurried up one ramp, then down the other and found the contact point on that side.

"Weave," Darcy pointed toward the poles.

I went through them as if I had the fastest cow in the world in front of me and shot onto the table.

"Down!" Darcy's voice called.

Tucking my paws under me, I dropped.

"One..." Dr. Wilson began to count.

I looked around to get my barring. The teeter totter was next.

"...two..."

Weariness washed through me. My tongue felt dry and I gasped for air.

"...three," Dr. Wilson chanted.

"Hang in there, Belle," roared Buster.

"…four . . . five."

"Belle, teeter-totter," Darcy pointed.

I forced myself off the table and ran. Pausing only long enough to place my paw in the correct spot, I started to climb. Up and up I went.

Crowd smells grew faint, and I lost track of its murmuring. Seeing nothing but the board in front of me, I climbed into stillness.

When would the teeter fall? Slowing my step, I glanced left and right to make sure I was in the middle of it. But the ground was so far down. A shiver raced through me and I stopped.

"You can do it, Belle." Painter's faint bark reached me.

Darcy's electric smell wafted close. A quick sniff told me she had managed to hobble in front of the teeter totter. She'd be there to meet me.

If she could function right now, so could I.

I took another step, and then another.

Whoosh! Down I dropped. Air rushed by. The ground rose. *Wump!* The teeter hit the ground. Darcy's smell engulfed me. I opened my eyes to find her in front of me.

Thank you dog heaven. I marched straight toward her. As I stepped to the ground, she pointed left.

"Jump, Belle."

My legs shook, and my sides heaved. Gasping, I gathered aching muscles for the first leap. As I cleared the bar and landed, the pads under my feet burned. I flung myself over the second jump, just clearing it.

Oh dog heaven, one more. I've got to do it.

The final jump's slats gleamed. Every muscle straining, I hurled myself toward it.

My breath tore at my throat, and my mouth felt like I'd been eating sand. I can't do it. I'm going to fall right on that last jump.

"Clear it! Clear it!" Cheri barked.

"Go Belle! Go Belle!" Painter, Buster, and even King thundered.

Behind me, Darcy smelled like a thousand thunderstorms about to burst.

Come, strength, come. I strained to gather speed. Ready. Set. Leap.

A spurt of energy shot me into the air. I floated, as if in a dream, the white fence hovering below me.

Would my hind legs clear it? They felt like dead branches dangling from my hips.

The bar vanished from view. My front feet touched the earth. I waited for the thud of a falling fence. Instead my back paws plopped into the dirt. I staggered to the finish line and sat.

A roar exploded from the crowd. King, Painter, Buster, and Cheri woofed.

Darcy hobbled up and put on my tab, tears streaming down her face. I cowered, fearing I'd messed up bad without knowing it. But she smiled at me as she wiped her eyes.

"Good dog, Belle, good dog. You did it."

I did it! I finished the class, did my best to try to win. I'd even managed to get on and off that flea bitten teeter-totter. Lifting my tail and ears, I held my head high.

"Ladies and Gentlemen," Dr. Wilson spoke above the noise. "Belle and Darcy Simmons ran the course in 59 seconds. That ties them time-wise with Cheri and her handler J. J. Rogers."

The crowd roared.

Holy dog biscuits. I'd not only completed the class, I'd done as well as the best dog in it.

"However," Dr. Wilson continued. "Cheri had a minor fault. Belle..."

My ears and tail dropped. Here came the final judgment. I saw Margaret looking at Darcy from the stands.

"Belle didn't get a single fault. Congratulations to Belle and Darcy for a perfect run, our new grand champion team."

Barks and cheers erupted.

Shivers ran through me. I not only finished the class, I finished off the competition. And I was good. Really good.

Balancing on her good leg, Darcy scooped me in her arms.

I washed her face and neck.

Dr. Wilson handed her a purple ribbon longer than I was tall.

J. J. got the red, white and blue Reserve Champion award.

Darcy put me down. We left the arena and met Buster, Toby, Aunt Ellen, Painter, Margaret and Uncle Jim by the Pooch Patrol stall.

Toby shook Darcy's hand. "Belle sure came a long way, didn't she?"

Uncle Jim looked at him and then at Darcy. "So have a couple of humans, I think. Good job, all of you."

Darcy looked at her ribbon. "Well, I guess that means Belle stays with us, right Mom?"

Margaret laughed. "Yes, I guess we're stuck with her."

"And now Buster gets to go home, too," said Uncle Jim. "Painter's almost well, and Toby can work with him for next year."

Buster was coming home. I nuzzled him.

Toby looked sad. "I'll miss you boy."

"I'll bring him over when I bring Belle to practice." Darcy said. She smiled at J. J. "I'll see you at the state 4-H agility trials."

J. J. laughed. "That'll be fun. It was a good match today."

I looked at Cheri. "How do you feel about being second?"

She wagged her tail. "I'm still going to state fair. Who knows what will happen then. There might be dogs who perform better than we do. Or you and I might battle it out again."

"My turn this time, yours next, maybe." I said.

"That's the way agility goes," she answered.

We nuzzled each other. Then J. J. led Cheri away, the red-white-and-blue ribbon fluttering from her belt.

Darcy shifted her weight and lifted her injured foot off the ground.

Uncle Jim steadied her "You're a trooper." He grinned at everyone. "What do you say we drop Buster and Belle off, get Bob, and go for pizza. My treat."

Toby and Darcy looked at each other and laughed. "You don't need to ask us twice," said Toby.

Nothing ever felt as soft as the grass when Darcy let me into the back yard a while later. I lay down and let her rub my belly.

"Come on Darcy. We're ready to go," called Margaret from the human den.

Darcy looked toward the back door. "Should I lock the doggie door?"

I held my breath.

"No," replied Margaret smiling. "Let's leave it open. We'll see if she can ignore the kitchen waste basket."

I wagged my tail to promise the garbage pail would stay up right. I have better things to do than tip it over.

Darcy went inside

I joined Buster under a tree.

He wiggled his nose in greeting then closed his eyes.

I clay down and cuddled against him.

Darcy, Margaret, and Bob's steps echoed in the front of the human den. They got into the car and drove off. The smell of the water that made the car go lingered.

After a while, the aroma of grass replaced it, punctuated by the odor of squirrels beyond the fence.

Head on my paws, I enjoyed odors. Soon Darcy and I would be practicing for the state trials. If I concentrated, I could handle the course they presented. Holy dog biscuits, I could hardly wait.

ABOUT THE AUTHOR

Connie Gotsch based the character of Belle on her dog Kiri. This book is her second novel staring Belle. She's written two other books for grown-ups, the suspense/thriller *Snap me a Future*, and the mainstream/ romance *A Mouth Full of Shell*, both available at her web site www.conniegotsch.com

A resident of Farmington, New Mexico, Connie works for KSJE, Public Radio for the Four Corners serving as Program Director, hosting the award-winning morning classical music show, "Roving with the Arts," and producing a segment for authors called "Write On Four Corners." In cooperation with the Farmington Public Library, she creates the story time program, "Cuentos Hahne and Tales" for kids and kids at heart. She produces award-winning arts documentaries and arts interviews. In 2007, New Mexico Press Women named her their Communicator of Achievement.

Reach Connie where Imagination's on Board at cgotsch@gobrainstorm.net

LaVergne, TN USA
30 October 2010
202874LV00002B/2/P